About the Author

George Hobson is a priest in the Episcopal/Anglican Church. He has lived in France for over half his life, working with both French and English-speaking churches. He studied theology at Oxford in the 1980s and earned his doctorate in 1989. With his wife, Victoria, he has travelled extensively in developing countries, teaching courses in theological colleges. He has published two books of poetry in England: *Rumours of Hope*, with Piquant Editions, and a collective volume, *Forgotten Genocides of the 20th Century*, with Garod Books. His poem "Sun-Patch" won Second Prize in the International Bridport Poetry Competition in 1995.

Faces of Memory

George Hobson

Faces of Memory

Olympia Publishers
London

www.olympiapublishers.com
OLYMPIA PAPERBACK EDITION

Copyright © George Hobson 2017

The right of George Hobson to be identified as author of
this work has been asserted in accordance with sections 77 and 78
of the Copyright, Designs and Patents Act 1988.

All Rights Reserved

No reproduction, copy or transmission of this publication
may be made without written permission.
No paragraph of this publication may be reproduced,
copied or transmitted save with the written permission of the
publisher, or in accordance with the provisions
of the Copyright Act 1956 (as amended).

Any person who commits any unauthorised act in relation to
this publication may be liable to criminal
prosecution and civil claims for damage.

A CIP catalogue record for this title is
available from the British Library.

ISBN: 978-1-84897-843-0

First Published in 2017

Olympia Publishers
60 Cannon Street
London
EC4N 6NP

Printed in Great Britain

Dedication

For dear Victoria: wife of my youth, soul-mate, companion through life.

Acknowledgments

I am immensely grateful to the Apichella family for their love and friendship over the years: Michael, Judy, Maria, Lizzie, Caroline, Francesca, and Michael jr. Their belief in me as a poet, their unflagging support, their lucid insights, their lively faith, have sustained me more than they will ever know. Maria, a gifted poet herself, has encouraged and guided me generously over the years; Michael, writer, teacher, painter, teller of hilarious tales, has stood by my side as a friend through thick and thin; and the rest of the family, with Judy holding the whole Apichella show together (no small feat), have wrapped their arms around me and Victoria with joyful affection, humour, and much laughter. This book owes more to them than I can say.

THE BELLS OF SWETTL

Now at seven, I sense that monks
At Swettl are gathering to dine. All nine
Come habited in brown to take their meal
In common in the hall, as bells in the tower bowl
Their sound down alleys of blue spruce,
Alleys where the grand trees stand sentinel
On time.
Swallows are wheeling in the pastel skies,
Turning, returning, weaving patterns
On the violet inviolate ancient cloth
Of heaven,
As bells in the high baroque tower
Of Swettl ring to call the monks to sit
At table in communion with each other
And their Lord.

I

I am not at Swettl now, nor know
For sure if monks still gather there to sup.
Do the nine I knew still greet the day with Lauds?
"O great earth, mass unimaginable,
Cloud-bearing ball propelled by God,
Vehicle to carry seas and continents
Through space, deploying time as you revolve:
O creature placed in heaven's carrousel,
Not you but Him who made you, we adore!
O singing sun, whom the birds at dawn
All herald as they greet the light!
Bright Poppy, princely flower in the field of sky,
Whom all our earthly flowers imitate:
Glorious beacon, friend of Life, image
Of the One who made you: *Him* we worship!"

But even now, before the blood-red sun
Arises splendid from below the earth,
Already in the mutter of the tree-combing wind,
In the chanting of doves, the psalmody of larks,

In the descant of insects stirred by dawn,
In the cock's wild day-declaring crow
That cracks the heavy night and wakes the world;
Already in the stillness of the waiting hills,
In the silence of the kindled clouds,
I hear the murmur and reverberation,
The echo, the annunciation,
The summons and coming thunder
Of Eternal Life.

II

Thanksgiving is the ground of our communion,
Praise the articulation of our hope.
Now at Swettl, now and always while I live,
The monks sing Matins as the bridegroom sun
Comes shouldering his way between the hills
To set the night-logged spruce aflame,
The sentinel spruce, custodians of time past.
In the mirror of the inner eye
The woods of former years burn bright.
Light-shafts buttress forests rooted
In a thousand thousand mornings.
In the cobalt shade of countless days, bright
Sun-pools shine among the cool deep fern
Of numberless forgettings.
Strokes of light on leaning pine-trunks
Blaze trails overgrown by pain,
By thorn and bracken,
Trails cleared back in boyhood
Before the weather turned,
Before the darkening,

The recompense and reckoning,
Before the ladder to the tree-house broke,
Before the landmark of the Twisted Oak
Came crashing in a January storm
Across the old trail home.

Bells long still now toll
In the spiralled ear:
Bells of my antiquity are echoing.
With memory's perfect pitch I hear
True tones made pure by distance,
Concentrate of former days
Refined in time's alembic. Now
The bells of Swettl gong, gong-gong,
Backward, forward, echoing,
Tintinabulations in the inner ear,
In the heart's private rooms,
Intimating former times and times that are to be.
Like fragrance by the apple tree,
Like hummingbirds above the columbine.

Our past is echo of our present
And image of the age to come.

III

Each present moment is both seed and crop,
A planting and a gathering in;
It holds the pit and tuber and the buried bulb,
The waiting and maturing and the sudden bloom.
Everything is happening *now*.
The day stands forth with vigour,
The world goes off to work.
At Swettl the canonicals of Terce are sung.
"Morning!" the lusty bells ring out.
"Heat and light are born! Hope is here!"
The sun's hand is resting on our hair.

We head to market with our wares,
Fruit of all our days and nights,
Of all the hours of earth's extended tour
Among the stars.
Now we sell the seed of fruit to come,
When the morning of today will be a long time gone.
Time is not a medium we move in,
Not a river bearing chips downstream,

But a fabric of relations and decisions,
Of motions of the mind and heart and tongue
Towards oneself and others and towards God,
Today.

The bells of Swettl call me now
To face the piercing sun.
"Recall the times, the times, recall..."
When I stoned a hissing tomcat in an alley
When I thrashed a boy who beat me in a game
When I cursed a man who laughed at me in public
When I stabbed my aging father with my tongue
When I pushed aside a colleague for my profit
When I let a friend be slandered by his foes
When I took my neighbour's wife with cool indifference
When I gloated at the failure of a rival
When I covered up misdoing with a lie
When I falsely put the blame on all the others—
On parents, spouse, the government and God—
For the violence of my own embittered heart.

Drag out all the decomposing bodies
In the bushes by the railroad tracks
Where the transcontinental used to thunder by
And bury pain behind the noise

And bury guilt beneath the steam (or seem to)
And hold out the offer of atonement
By flight across the open plains.
Exhume the corpses in the cellar,
Rotting in the hard-packed ground
Beneath the bottles of Nuits-St-Georges
Aligned along the wall in racks.
Open up the closets full of tears,
The cupboards stuffed with rage,
The boxes crammed with IOUs:
Fetch all these into the sun,
Call them out of hiding:
Own them yours.
Each morning is a time to turn,
To pull weeds, disc old sod, sow seed:
A time to welcome light.
We labour under guilt
And plod towards death;
God's judgement is upon us
For deeds undone and done.
Soul, bow; bend low the knee;
Ask forgiveness and forgive.
Then rise, stand tall:
For under grace,
By God's Word offered once and now,

You live.

God reigns
God has come
Have mercy on us, Father

He is coming

Oh, hear the bells of Swettl pealing:
"Time is made of times, of times..."
Listen to them gong:
"Make up the time, the time..."
Swallows are looping in the radiant air,
Figuring patterns on the blue,
Patterns of hope.
Then and tomorrow and forever
Are now:
Everything is happening today.

IV

Sext is sung at noon to celebrate
High day, when shadows of our boundary stones
No longer stain the soil like Abel's blood.
The column of the dial points only up,
The sky is white with heat, the animals
Are resting in the shade and flicking flies.
No cock crows now, denial is behind,
Not Peter's past nor mine can echo
In this present. Not even chickens squawk.
Old dogs lie sprawled like grainsacks in the court.

I hear a gong from long ago
The chime is ringing
The lunch-gong chiming from the cabin door
(O Canada! Canada!):
It lifts across the willows by the creek,
Carries past the cattle chute,
Along the snake-rail fence,
Down to where the sweet wild berries grow
And where the clover's thick,

The air as clear as glass,
Full of insect sounds and silence;
Down to stubbled fields where son and father
Stand by leaning bales, hay-hooks in hand,
And squint through heavy heat of noon,
Out of time,
At the far-off, shaggy, darkly shining edge
Of the evergreen forest of the North.

Run, little boy,
Run down the riverbank,
Go where the willows grow,
And fetch some home.

Quickly, my joy,
Find where the reeds grow rank,
Where the creek runs slow,
And fetch some home.

Hurry, bright boy,
Go where the lank
Rushes bend and winds blow,
And fetch some home.

I'll make a toy,
A boat of reeds from where we drank
In cold streams long ago:
You'll fetch it home.

A wreath, sweet boy,
I'll fashion: a golden crown
To set upon your head:
And God will fetch you home.

Heavenly Father,
Holding us in the hollow of your hand:
Hallowed be your Name!
In the heat beating on the rock of our years,
Pressing the dry stone walls of our days,
Stones laid on stones,
We know your love's weight,
Your heart's fierce fire!
Out of your mind's inconceivable kiln,
Fired by unimaginable Joy,
Have we come forth, and all this blaze and pageant,
This crackle and tumult of creatures,
Now all still at midday.
Oh, what sun-falls,
What seas of light!

The air like honey of acacia,
The heat like wagon-loads of straw.
Sod, leaf, bush, stone,
Brown, buff, gold, green–
All burning!
At your core all is still.
You burn.
You distill, like memory.
You consume our chaff.
Redemptor!
Like poppies flaming in oatfields,
You are molten, glowing.
In eyes full of longing you blaze
Like Bethlehem's star.
All these are gleamings of Love,
Out-shinings of Life in Joy.
Here in heat,
In this revel of stillness,
You speak.
Holy God!
In this moment of time out of time
(You are *Present*),
I hear.
Lord–my Lord!
Hallowed be your Name.

V

Now there is a waning in the power of our hand.
The monks chant None with shorter breath than Terce.
They no longer leap up to sing the psalms;
Their backs ache, leaning in the stalls.
Bodies, less pliant than once,
Mark their own antiphonal complaint:
They tell of falls and fractures,
Sprains, twists,
The softening of muscles,
The hardening of arteries:
A loss of suppleness.
They tell of illness and infection,
Operations,
The surgeon's knife and stitches,
Scars:
A sense of diminishing capacity.
They tell of bruises to the soul,
Wounds from enemies and friends,
The blows of disappointment;
Of moral weakness,

Blindness,
Cruelty:
The heart's corruption.

It is another time:
The beginning of the coming to terms with the end.
We travel on the far side of noon now,
The descent has begun.
Below us lies the valley of temptation,
Where the devil prowls and the Lord God
Puts to the test.
The rush of sap, the flowering,
The swell of buxom foliage,
All that is past:
Summer is closing,
The edges of the leaves are turning brown.

Weariness accompanies the ripening fruit.
We are vulnerable, open to temptation:
Is God good?
Will the Lord, after all, have mercy?
Does He really call us by our name?
O Christ—we doubt!
Show us your love!
Make known to us your power!

"No sign shall be given but the sign of Jonah."

We are anxious, open to deception:
Does death, after all, mark the end?
Shall the wicked not be judged,
Justice not be done,
Shall faith prove illusion,
Truth a lie?
Shall the Living God not greet us
Beyond the grave?

*"I am the Resurrection and the Life:
He that believes in me, though he die,
Yet shall he live."*

We are fearful, open to delusion:
Are men not simply beasts that think?
Are they not merely reasoning machines,
Fortuitous configurations of matter?
Have they not got the power, right and freedom
To determine their own being
And establish their rule?
At the altar where proud men worship the Lie,
Bewitching idols hiss:

"Humanity is nature's end and sum:
God's image:
God."

A voice strikes my ear:
"I am the Truth,
The Lord who made all things,
Who alone stretched out the heavens,
Who spread out the earth by myself.
I will not give my glory to another
Or my praise to idols."

"Fear not!
I am the Alpha and the Omega,
The Living One that was dead.
Behold, I am alive forevermore!"

Fatigue may lure us into boredom
Or ensnare us with the drug of resignation;
It may provoke impetuous decisions,
Self-pitying recriminations,
The spring-back of held-down resentment,
Octobers pretending to be May.

No buds blossom in the gardens of regret

The shadows of the spruce are turning eastward,
We cannot turn them back.
In the deepening shade
Eyes beckon, mock.

My God! My God!

He comes!
My Saviour!
My ears prick up like a stag's
At the snap of a twig in the woods.
Oh, praise, praise, praise!
His fingers touch my eyes,
The veil draws back,
The spell lifts—
Immanuel!

"My Lord and my God!"

A Voice speaks to my heart:
*"If the Son sets you free,
You will be free indeed."*

The monks with straightened backs are chanting None;
The sun slants down,
The time-worn stalls are shot with gold.
"O kindly Lord,
By grace through your dear Presence
In the Holy Spirit with us,
Now and always,
We shall not fail to follow you to darkness
And the grave.
We bless you, Lord,
For you shall raise us with you
To the Father.
May your Name be praised forever!"

Before the subsiding and the last beginning,
There is much to do.
Nor is it humdrum:
Nothing is humdrum but death.
Shall we not cultivate?
Shall we not reap what we have sown?
Our meaning lies in what our end will be.
Body, be strong! Soul, keep hope!
The harvest rains will come!

VI

We have put order in the wild world.
We have cleared the ground on our allotted space,
Enclosed primeval land, felled woods,
Made houses, fields, walls, and carved out lives
Among the thorns and thistles and the stony ground
Of the high places of the world, beside the rubble
Of eroded mountains and the green hills
And ancient rivers on the valley floors.
Our hands have done all this amidst the chiming
Days, time's bells, God's carillon:
Days that have rung the changes on our works,
Providing them a frame to find their shape in,
Shaping us as we perform them,
Then bearing them away into the past
While carrying us who do them up the stream
Against death's turgid current, towards
The Land where change, a leaping fountain,
Is renewal, and the Lord of time,
Our Saviour, shall show our sculpted souls
To be the goal of His own mighty Work.

Oh, the bells have tolled our hours through the years!
With the huddled woods we've borne the wind's fists,
Suffered brain-bewildering fog and winter's
Whetted knife; with earth and leaf we've crumpled
Under summer drought, peered into skies
Blank as pages, quailed at the sight
Of clouds floating, bloated, impotent,
Like sad-eyed eunuchs on parade.
But we've known as well the lavish turbulence
Of thick snow streaming out of heaven,
White on white,
The anarchy of whirling flakes,
Lace on lace,
The blessing of disorderly order,
Kiss on kiss:
The Father's regenerative breath
Condensing on His world
And on our human shaping
And misshaping,
On all our shame,
Summoning being to humility
And the immaculate order of grace.

And now is Vespers. Quiet.
The rains have come, the troupes of drops

Have danced across the property of God.
Earth, wet, glad, gurgles;
Soil, scrubbed, drenched, drains.
The continent of cloud
Is breaking into islands,
Tinted archipelagoes
That imitate the hills:
Old companions, yoked in space,
Folded together at creation.
All now are darkening under heaven:
Gold gone, red gone,
Shape in-the-round gone:
Silhouettes sharpening,
Cut-outs,
Tracery,
Pen-and-ink imaginings,
Cross-hatchings,
Blocks of opal in the dusk.
Before the monks have done
And Evensong is sung,
The hills and clouds,
Like a couple in their age,
Link arms and retire into night.

Whom do I see walking in the twilight?
Who stands on Eighty-Second Street and Park,
New York City? Cosmopolitan
Lady: fur coat, velvet, silk:
Full lips, a Jewish beauty's skin:
Eyes the colour of the pale wind that blows
Through Canaletto's Venice, where gondolieri
Greet their ladies passing on the Grand Canal.

This lady is my mother,
Her heart contains a *grand amour*
(He was not my father).
She lived in Paris in the Thirties, he was French
(My mother's mother, twice wed, disapproved).
Together they discovered love,
The delights of intimate encounter:
A sense of being known;
Often they watched the moon over St. Sulpice,
Blithe stone statues in the Luxembourg Gardens,
Plane trees in livery on the banks of the Seine,
Chestnuts sailing up the Champs de Mars:
Of being understood;
In summer they sat outside cafés
And drank Italian vermouth
And watched the waiters bob like penguins;

In winter they sat in bistros
And smelt garlic and roasted coffee beans
And ate escargots and coq au vin:
Of being claimed;
They saw snow on the boulevards in January,
Snow on the steep roofs and mansards,
A white cape over Notre Dame,
Ermine on the Pont St. Michel,
Silver ice on the Quai du Louvre:
Of being seen;
One evening in May they were caught
In a rainstorm over Montparnasse;
Soaked to the skin,
They took off their shoes
And ran barefoot through the flooded streets,
Laughing:
Of being loved.
Oh, love's high yearning,
Echo of heaven,
Sweet hurry to marry,
A hunger, a hoping:
Herald of Joy!

One summer night in Normandy,
While the green land breathed quietly,

Came news of the crash
Of the motorcycle crash
The crash on the road to Bolbec
Between Yvetot and Bolbec
On the winding road to Bolbec
Bolbec.

Sans retour, sans retour

She knows (she learned)
You can't live yesterday.
She fled back to America,
To the City born tomorrow:
And fiercely repressed self-pity,
And ruthlessly stanched the pain,
And bitterly barricaded Europe
Behind the hard angularities
And rough-edged visions
Of the future-oriented Brave New World.

Who stands on the corner of Eighty-Second and Park?
I ask you, Vespers ending: whom do I meet
Here? Whom join, with my half-brother,
In her impeccable New York apartment, where Keats
And Guy de Maupassant stand flanked by jades

And Sèvres porcelains and Chinese lacquer bowls?
She sits on her upholstered sofa smoking,
A lonely lady contemplating dusk,
Who hasn't read *Le Lac* or *La Mort du Loup*
In fifty years. Beneath a Boucher drawing
Of women round a hearth, and two French
Prints entitled *Vue d'une Fontaine Antique*
And *Vue de L'Intérieur d'une Ferme,*
She peers with enigmatic gaze into the evening
(In a tower block above Manhattan's bedlam),
Accompanied by sons and stepsons
And gentlemen of varied ages
(But not by any former husband),
Who stare from photographs in leather frames
Grouped atop her *Empire* desk
And handsome *Louis Quinze* end-tables
In-laid with mother-of-pearl.
Whom do I see here
As I peer at her from the pictures
Of my mother's first-born son?
Who is this lady smoking in the twilight?

Remember, Mummy, when we crossed the Atlantic
(New York to Le Havre took a week)?
Remember our talk in that empty compartment

On the Night Express from Paris to Lausanne?
We've shared many meals together, haven't we,
    In this country or in that, over the years,
    Seeking each other across the dinner table,
        Mother and son?
And then there are the memories of boyhood,
      The last summer on Long Island,
    The waves rolling in off Southampton:
        You were young still,
        Beautiful still,
        I just a stripling,
    My half-brother barely out of diapers.
        Underneath appearances
        I knew you were sad;
The marriage you'd contracted at War's end
        Was dead
(So had the first one been, ten years earlier,
  So would the next one be, ten years on).
      O Mother, hear me:
How should I, so young, have given comfort
And brought the consolation of a husband?
  No child can be a parent's confidant.
    Hear me further: I speak with love
(Christ's blood has long since washed away
      My grief and accusation):

How could you, so wounded,
Who had not known a mother's warmth yourself,
Have given me the tenderness you lacked?

Ah, Mother, let us walk together
In the peace of Jesus, reconciled by grace,
Beyond the terrors of the unloved heart,
Under the blessing of the Father through the Son.
The storms are passed. The blue flag is flying
On the Beach Club pole, the red one is down.
Let us walk on the beach and pick up shells,
Smell the salt in the wind off the sea,
See the wet kelp gleaming like polished horn
On the sand, the disconsolate algae
Strewn in the sun, beside the whelks
And surf-singing conches and the broken clams.
The grey gulls wheel above the waves,
I hear them in my mind's ear screeching;
They ride the breakers and the dark-bellied clouds
Clearing westward, they turn above the houses
Standing in the dunes and pointy beach grass,
Bleached grey houses faced with shingles
That rise up on the far-off shores of memory,
Fronting the inveterate sea.

Here we shall walk, you and I,
Arm in arm as evening claims us,
Mother and son.
The office of Vespers is finished,
The day is done;
The years have rolled over us like waves,
We are ready to rest.
The Father takes us in His tenderness,
His ensign over us is love;
The Spirit folds us in His mercy,
Under the descending Dove.

But look! In the haze of dusk and ocean,
Suddenly my earthly father's presence
Stands beside us on the watery strand.
I see nothing, only sense his company,
Even as I hear down the darkening beachfront
The breakers booming and the intermittent
Rush up the sand and retreat of the wash.
My mother grows fearful, remembering
My father's wild side to the fore
When they were married. She grips my arm and bends
Her pale Venetian eyes upon my face.
"Can you love me?" she seems to ask. I stare.
Her gaze is unrelenting. "Can you?" I nod,

Tearful. She weeps. Then a yielding:
She lets go something, accepts something else:
Her grip relaxes.
Mother, are you letting go your life?
Are you owning it yours?
Not the life you wanted or imagined,
But the life you really lived,
On earth and under heaven?
My mother's eyes say: "Yes."
The sense of the presence of my father fades.
I hear the pounding sea
And seagulls crying,
And know suddenly,
With a leap in my heart,
That the slap and thump
Of the breaking waves
Is praise: the planet's applause
For its Redeemer King.
O Mother, O Father, hear me: one day
We shall know each other perfectly
(As God has always known us perfectly),
In Christ's Kingdom that is coming
(Christ's Kingdom here already by the Spirit):
His Kingdom come.

VII

Now night is here. The monks with candles, cowls
Pulled up against the cold, steal from their beds
And down the stairway to the choir, their shadows wobbling
On the bare stone walls, to offer Compline
To the Sovereign Lord of heaven, earth, and hell,
To Him who makes and unmakes, sole God,
Creator, just Judge of all the world,
The Alpha and the Omega, who wills to offer mercy
To the merciful and to the mercy-seeking:
"O thrice-blessed gracious Saviour—
Father, Son and Holy Spirit—
Hear our prayer!
Lord, sustain us!
Take not your hand from ours
At this our exodus
And last sea-crossing;
Deliver us from death,
O Powerful Redeemer,
And lead us through this Night
To everlasting Day!"

Now we are entering darkness,
Where the river dives under the mountain.
The goats clamber over the wall,
The starlings fly up from the lime-trees.
In the tower the bells ring fainter,
The sound of the gong dies away.
Does the air by the spring in the hollow
Still smell of mint and musk?
Do bees still hum in the silence?
Do dragonflies glint in the light?
Oh, we do not hear the thrushes singing any longer,
Nor see the swallows weaving patterns
On the violet inviolate cloth of heaven;
The hoot and float of the owl
In the haunted woods of childhood
Is an ancient dream.

Remembrance is past

If the moon still lies like an oyster shell
On the table of night,
And the stars are scattered like pearls
On the satin cloth,
I see it so no longer,

Nor know to fit my tongue to sight.
Earthly eyes and speech have done.
Neither object nor image,
Sense nor symbol,
Neither science nor poetry,
Has purchase on reality any more:
Death turns sign and reference both to dust.
Our lives have flown out of the frame.
Fearless, we hang by Wrath's Fire,
Saved by heavenly grace from judgement,
Joined to the Holy Spirit brooding
On the seat of God's Final Assize.
The Lord's Word goes forth in power:
In a twinkling the might of His Name
Bears up our hearts to His Bower
And dooms bleak Death to the Flame.
For here in the Void we meet our Saviour,
The Truth and the Way to God the Father,
Who once took human flesh and form
And dwelt with us on earth in time.
He bore our dereliction on the blasted Tree,
He gave His life for ours on Calvary,
And by the blood He shed in pain,
He frees our souls from guilt and shame
And bids us welcome in His Family.

"We cry to you, O Father God,
We who weep with those who mourn,
Who lift to you the suffering of creatures fallen:
Grant that justice may be done,
That mercy may be shown to them,
Alive or dead or still unborn,
Whose hearts choose Life,
That we and those we pray for, may,
Like the thief you welcomed on the Cross,
Be found today in Paradise."

"O God, our Maker and Redeemer,
We have remembered you
In all our comings and our goings;
In all our celebrations
We have invoked your Holy Name;
In our brief span of mortal life
We have delighted in your Beauty.
Remember us, O King of kings,
Give grace,
Exchange our rags for robes of righteousness:
Not ours but Christ's.
Wanderers inglorious,
Prone to dissolution:

Grant us, O God, when the last trumpet sounds,
To rise with radiant bodies,
The prize of our Lord's triumph
And dwell with you forever in your Kingdom."

Communion with the Living Word awaits us,
When immediate knowledge shall be the fruit of Love;
For we shall see Him face to face in all His Beauty,
God's Glory,
Christ,
Our true being's true Lover:
We shall see Him as He is,
Resplendent, tender:
Gentle Lord!
Just King!
Fear will flee away,
Guilt roll back,
Pride shrivel,
As furrowed brows,
Bent bodies,
Broken hearts,
Are loosed from pain
And oppressing sin,
The grief of shattered dreams.
Oh, we shall be wholly open to the Light,

And we shall worship Christ in Joy,
And He will make us like Himself.
We have sometime tasted conviviality
(A kind of communion)
In a present long past,
Now nearly forgotten;
We shall know its fulfilment
In the company of Heaven,
In Life Eternal,
In a love perfected
Through total surrender.

Christ has died, Christ has risen

For now, we are under the mountain

"A crown of victory
Is waiting for you,
And God will fetch you home."

God remembers us

Christ will come again

By hope in Him we live, now and always

He is faithful who promised

The sap that drove our days
And moved our tongues and hands
Has jelled to amber;
Time lies flat behind us
Like a steamer's wake.
The foam thrown up by life in spate
Has turned to marble;
The tattoos on the sea's bruised skin
Have paled like ink on letters in old trunks.
The churned green goes to indigo,
To midnight blue,
To slate,
Until all traces of the steamer's passage vanish.

The ship has slipped over the edge of the sea

God holds us fast

The plunge of the gull, the splash in the water,
The daring Bird devours the fish;
The hurtling train, the hole in the mountain,
The Locomotive consumes the cliff.

Convoy of cars, mustered by Christ,
Claimed back at tunnel's end by Light;
In luminous triumph from darkness emerging,
Warrior-Day has defeated Night.

Sailboats passing, triangular patches,
Countless varieties coursing in sea-wind,
Singing in land-breeze by pebble-brown
Coastlines, by crocodile headlands,
Past remnants of cliff-face fissured by surf.
Some come a-cropper, off-course diverging,
Drifting in fog, on hidden reefs grounding,
Abused by the sea-swell and howling typhoon;
Others in the middle of open sea slackening,
Becalmed in confusion, idle, float, waiting,
Boiled by hot oceans, bedevilled by torment
Of sea-snakes up bow-sides contorting
And coiling, on sun-baked decks writhing.
These know remorse without turning:
World-sorrow, rainless, windless,
Beyond grief, pain-toughened, tearless,
Weakened by fear, by evil beguiled
Into doubt and despair, the doldrums of sinful
Self-hatred, bitterness leading to death.
They lie on the ocean's flat surface,

Listless; on the motionless waters, broken,
Their keels cracked by contrary currents,
Tillers snapped, steering wheels fractured,
Rudders ripped up from their places
By wave-shock and riotous storm.

But—what is happening? Gracious God!
A wind comes rising in the East—
Oh, blow, grace-gusts! Blow, trumpet of pardon!
To each boat the bellows of Love!
Tighten slack sheets, swell sails,
Change larvae to butterflies,
Summon dull worms to glory!
All sizes count, all styles, all
Shapes of hull and canvas: all are called!
Oh, may they answer! May all tilt to windward!
Look–masts are canting, spars leaning!
Helms pitch, decks rock!
All roll in the movement of waters,
All stream under billows, surge forward,
Beating the sea's swell in rhythm,
By winds and tides carried and guided.
Each boat is beautiful, singular,
Ploughing its own path, peculiar,
Yet bound to all others forever

By one love and longing and goal!

Holy, Holy, Holy,
Lord God Almighty,
Heaven and earth are full of your glory!

The mountain has vanished
The ocean is gone

"I am the Living One; I was dead,
And behold I am alive for ever more!"

We've emerged from the tunnel
We've crossed the sea
We've come to Love's Fountain
To the One-in-Three

Holy, Holy, Holy

A High Gate towers on a windy Hill,
Half a mile high,
Oh, half a mile high and bloody!
The Gate is a Cross in a pointed Arch,
The Arch like hands in prayer,
Like bending Forms that share

A Loss and lean their weight
Upon the rough-hewn Cross, the Gate,
All bloody on the windy Hill.
Bereaved, the Figures mourn the Son,
Father and Spirit grieve the One
Forsaken for the sake of men:
My God laments His Loss,
He weeps upon the Cross.

Holy, Holy, Holy

Do you hear the cry go up?

"Salvation belongs to our God,
Who sits on the throne,
And to the Lamb!"

Who is the Lamb?

"The Lord, the King of Glory,
He is the Lamb,
The Lamb that was slain."

I see now all across a somber plain,
Turbid legions of humanity hobbling,

The crippled, outcast, tormented, stumbling,
Shoals of tatterdemalion persons,
Rank on rank of homeless humans
Fleeing the planet's civil war:
Disembowelled, stabbed,
Raped, abused,
Betrayed, shot,
Beheaded, burnt,
Starved, dismembered,
Despised, ignored,
Abandoned, mocked, rejected.
Most are ordinary men and women,
With no illusions of innocence
Or claims to honour,
Yet not lacking in dignity,
Not lacking in
Beauty.
Each once was an infant
With skin like porcelain
And soft flesh like a mango.
All carry memories that howl in the night,
Hopes that were flung on the back of the wind,
Longings for love that were buried in stone.
Yet, here and there, even these,
Even these,

Show splashes of sun
On the flanks of their lives,
Flecks of felicity pointing to Joy.
All grieve Adam's Fall
And suffer Cain's evil.
Each seeks a Home:
To love, be loved,
To know, be known:
To be free.

Each thirsts for upwelling fountains,
For freshets tumbling down mountains,
For streams that burble on mossy stones
And pools where fish sleep among reeds;
For rivers of azure plaited like ribbons
In the tresses of meadows and the green braids of valleys;
For fields of iris and poppies blooming
In the radiant, gold-foil-flashing Morning,
Where creatures ever make revelry
In luminous immortality.
Here Beauty never fades,
Nor creature dies;
Prospect opens onto prospect
In perfect order and surprise.

Such thirsting is the recollection,
Image, anticipation
Of the Sabbath Rest of God's Creation,
The Seventh Day of the world.
As in an hour-glass each grain of sand,
Passing from the place of measured time
To the place of rest, must drop from the upper chamber
Through a narrow strait to the sphere below,
So every person on the shell-pocked plain,
Beset by guilt and pain,
Must enter by the narrow Way
And climb the bare and bloody Tree,
If he would cross into the Holy Land
And pass into Eternity.
I see the tens of billions move
Across the field of mud and hate
And funnel through the breach of blood
That breaks sin's curse and shatters fate.
We clamber up the splintered rood
And reach our arms around the stake
And feel the grain against our cheek
And hear the pulse-beat of his heart
Still thumping there inside the wood
For us.
We weep.

"Behold, the dwelling of God is with men.
He will wipe away every tear from their eyes,
And death shall be no more,
Neither shall there be mourning nor crying nor
Pain any more,
For the former things have passed away."

Cleaving to the blood-caked Cross,
I feel the massive trunk expand;
It swells into a mighty Tree
Reaching towards Infinity;
Its limbs thrust up to Heaven's dome
And bear the lost and wounded Home.

And now in light unimaginable
We become leaves innumerable
Covering the Perennial Tree
As it stands before God's Throne.
The Wind makes us shimmer,
We flutter, we murmur,
We applaud with deep ardour
At the sight of our King.
A hush stills our exulting
As we see the Son, dazzling,

Incandescent in splendour,
With thorns for a crown.
We look into the Face of God the Lord—
Brighter than the brightest snow-field
Under flaming sun—
We look into His Face—
And *Live!*
And we are changed!
Made whole!
In His eyes
We see our image as He made us,
In His Face
We see our peace.
We are become who we are.

And we who are leaves are now *wings*—
Now *birds!*
With a rush we explode from the Tree!
We fly up with a whirring and tumult,
A great bursting and clamour and roar!
Wings! Wings!
Oh, flight into blue!
We soar on the wild Wind of God,
We wheel,
Dip,

         Plunge—
         Climb!
          Soar!
        We sing!
      Wings! Wings!
          Blue!
        Oh, free!
      Free to love fully!
          Free!

And below us as we tumble and spin in the Heavens,
  We see the crystal River of our great Salvation
Flowing from beneath the wondrous Cross of Glory,
   Watering the Light-fields of the New Creation,
   Drowning every evil from our old rebellion,
            Healing every blight.
            Enfolded in One Spirit,
         We have union with the Father,
           Source and Origin and End;
              And with our Friend,
             God's Word, true Spouse,
         Who takes us to Himself as Bride
            To live forever at His side.

              What was is old

The old is passed away
All things are new

Amen, *Amen.*

*****

The monks don't gather any more at Swettl
To sing the Offices and worship their Creator,
For they have passed from shadows to the Sun,
From figures to the Solid—
They sit now in the very Presence of their Saviour.
Swettl and the whole old earth
Have been folded like a garment;
All truth and love that ever were
Have been lifted up in glory.
The monks take wine and the bread of Life
And feast with their Friend and Brother;
Music resounds in the Kingdom of God,
Laughter rolls through Heaven.
The Bridegroom smiles upon His Bride,
The Bride upon her Lord;
For her He shed His rank and blood,
Her love is His reward.

THE PSALTERY

I

Of the house where we gathered I remember nothing,
Only the room where we worshiped—
A room with bay windows—
And the dining room next door,
With food laid out to feed our bodies,
Wine to spark our talk,
Counterpart to the figures of his flesh and blood,
The bread and wine,
Shared in commemoration of our Saviour's
Life laid down for us
To flush from our soiled souls the race's mud,
From our weak lungs pneumonia's silt,
And so to give us breath and recreate us.
We gathered as members of Christ's Body
In that particular place, and even now,
A long time later, set apart by leagues
And years and death, wherever each of us
May join with others to give God thanks,
We celebrate our unity in him.

II

The psaltery, like moonlight, sings a soft song,
Spilling ripples, casting wide rings on memory's pond,
Fond recollections of communion and the life to be,
Of life as it is meant to be and will be,
Flecks of time,
The pluck of chords making phosphorescence in the water,
Notes dancing, notes celebrating this bright night
By conjuring what will never be again.
Memory turns night to day,
Light breaks oblivion's sway,
Old leaves rise from the drowned clay
Of the somnolent pond.
Awakened by the psaltery's art,
Figures, unsought, start
To speak inside the quickened heart,
Affirming the forgotten bond.
Recovery of things past
Floating in moon-flakes
Summoned by the gentle strings:

Image of the Holy Spirit's action
To make the past transparent to the present,
The present to the past,
Gathering them together into fullness
Both in time and out of time,
Bequeathing stillness within movement,
Movement within stillness.

III

We had a hard time of it sailing up the coast.
Fog thick as custard muffled the bonging of the buoys,
Made a clang close by seem two miles off.
Calm sea, just a breath of wind.
We sailed by chart and compass,
Seeing nothing but fog thick as custard,
Hearing nothing but the whoosh and slap of water on
the bow,
Now and then a buoy—
"Clang! Clang!"
Lord, were we grateful for those buoys!
They kept us sane.
We imagined rocks out there in the fog ahead of us:
Swirling shapes simulated reefs,
Cliffs rose up and toppled,
Islands loomed and melted.
I swear the fog was like putty,
Like clay in the hands of demons.
Why, if we'd had a mind, we could have turned pots!
Imagine—pots! Hah!

Oh yes, there were moments we thought we were going mad.
But we kept our heads.
I tell you, it was the buoys:
"Clang! Clang!"
The day was like night;
When real night came, it hardly made a difference.
Can you imagine?
Well, on we sailed, on on into night,
Night thick as glue.
The water hissed along the bow,
The sails were phantoms.
As for us, why—well—
I tell you, we were *shades*,
Shades in Hades.
Can you imagine?

And then suddenly, in seconds,
We broke clear of the fog.

The stars gleamed like flecks of mica
On the parapet of night;
The sky's black vault arched over us,
The air was clear as crystal,
The stars rang out like bells in a great cathedral

In some old European city.
At the same instant, a mile to port,
We spied a harbour at the tip of an island a-twinkle with lights,
A mirror of the gleaming night.
"We're saved!" we cried.
"Saved!
Hallelujah!"
Oh, believe me, it was like entering the world to come.

We anchored in the harbour and rowed to shore.
Sailors and townsfolk jammed the tavern.
As we entered, heads turned, a hush fell,
Forty pairs of startled eyes stared.
I guess we looked like ghosts come back from hell.
Then a man spoke: "Where you from?"
"Gloucester," I said.
"Uh-huh."
"We had a hard time of it coming up the coast," I said.
"The fog was thick as custard—like clay."
"Never seen the like," my mate put in.
"Couldn't see your hand before your face."
"If we'd had a wheel," I said, "we could have turned pots."
That did it. Everyone laughed and began to talk at once.

They plied us with questions.
We told the whole tale.
Then it was beer all around and we drank to the Saviour.
Midnight gone, we rowed back to the boat.
That night we dreamed of stars in the firmament of heaven
Ringing out like bells in the enormous night,
Cathedral bells calling us to worship the Redeemer,
Stars, bells—angels—!
All glorifying God.

IV

Plucking chords by the light of the moon,
I recall the lake where the wild loon
Crooned in the night to its mate
Afloat on the dark hill's image
Where it hung from the shoreline upside down
On the glittering water full of stars.

We were family and crossed the lake together.
My father handled the outboard,
My stepmother trolled for char.
She put weights on the line to go deep.
"Char swim deep," she said. "You have to put weights on the line."
We nodded. Trolling made her happy.
She never got a bite, but she never gave up.
"Someday I'll get my char," she said.
"When you reach the pearly gates," we said.
She laughed and put another weight on the line.

In the heart of the wilderness: Ormond Lake.
The lake was uncharted, but we were not lost:
We were family and crossed the lake together.
At the far end a stream poured out its water,
Fresh off the hills. Rods in hand,
The five of us waded upstream,
My father right down the middle, casting.
We caught enough fish to keep two people in trout
All winter long (stocking them in town
In the butcher's freezer, eighteen miles
From the Little Creek Ranch).
I can still hear the whiz of the line
As a trout takes the wet fly and runs:
Round eyes like washers, wide mouth, a flash
Of pink, a sharp tug, the line taut suddenly,
A zing, the line running, then a reeling
As the trout turns, a running again, the line
Cutting water like a knife, reel spinning,
Whiiiiiiz, reeling again, a dark shape in the water
Twisting, the rod bent double, a flapping—
And then a scoop of the net and it's in!
At Ormond Lake in the heart of the wilderness,
God provided food—fish.
God provided *fish*!

When we were done, we headed back across the lake.
My father handled the outboard,
My stepmother trolled for char.
She put weights on her line to go deep.
"Char swim deep," she said.
We nodded and smiled.
We knew she'd never catch a char,
But she was happy. This was wilderness,
But we were not lost. We were family
And crossed the lake together.

V

I have listened to the silence of the clouds
(What is so silent as a cloud?),
I have glimpsed the conclusion of things earthly
And time's dying fall in the life of creatures,
Each, like a cloud, coming to be and passing,
Moved by wind across the earth,
Each dragging its shadow under it,
Dark twin of light,
Companion and contradiction of matter,
Meaning death

I have listened to the chords of the psaltery
Lifting places from Lethe,
Particular places gathered by the alchemy of memory
Into a single trajectory through time:
Armenian churches in the Caucasus
Hunkered on outcrops of stone,
Bearing letters in their walls
Bespeaking faith and blood
In witness to the crucified One;

Rutted roads in Rwanda, gashed like skulls,
Riding the hills where banana leaves chatter
And wind strums the pale eucalyptus;
Kabul's riddled buildings sunk in dust,
The women like blue sails billowing with wind,
Eyes, like almond corks, afloat in their burkas,
Peering quizzically at a hostile world;
The syncopated coast of Crete,
Old hills stooped under heat, eroded
Like the steps of ancient stairs
By the flux and ebb of peoples;
Alpine snowfields at the St. Bernard pass,
Poking white fingers at the cold stars
Motionless in moonlight, where Napoleon's
Army and a thousand horses struggled
Two centuries ago through mud towards Marengo;
Caribbean beaches soaking in ocean,
Haloing islands where varieties of green
Bask under blank, boundless blue;
Mosaics of sky cut out by rooflines,
Tiling the shadows on Venetian canals,
Where gondolas in turtle-green light glide
Soundlessly or rock next to stone stairs
Rooted in the Adriatic's veins;
Classical Paris, Paris of boulevards,

City of kings, *philosophes*, tumbrels,
Where the sober and the sensual keep company,
Pollarded plane trees threaten heaven,
And geraniums and chimney pots throw
Orange confetti on the zinc-plated rooftops
And beige balconies of stone;
Oxford, its colleges drowned in time,
Where stillness indwells cobbled courtyards
And ages of thought lie woven in silence
Like the plaited reeds of baskets;
Brash New York, its offices and tower-
Blocks mirroring the fantasies of moguls,
The hallucinations of avid men;
America's prairies, rugs of gold,
Now quiet under sun, now, as clouds gather,
Thrashed by wind and the artillery of rain;
Canada's woods bracketing a continent,
Heaped on its rocky flanks like duvets,
Where lakes and rivers and wild rushing streams
Inlay the wilderness with azure.

All this I've seen

But I ask at this time,
In this present that grows heavy on my shoulders,

Where am I in that
Stone
Snow
Sand
In that dust
That green
On those orange roads that ran with blood
Those veins of sea I drifted on with my beloved in another time?
Those fantastical windows of Manhattan mirrored me once
I revelled in those tropical seas once
I heard the eucalyptus in Rwanda weeping in the night
I stood inside those Armenian churches once with my wife
and sobbed.
Is that African mud still on my hands?
Is that Caucasian tuff under my fingernails still?
Does the lava from the earth's bowels that shaped Armenia
Still run molten in my heart—
Or has it cooled and grown hard?

Do I grow old?

Do I still rage to think of cruel men murdering children?
Do I still mourn?
Do I truly grieve for my own sin and yours,
For humanity's corruption,
For the planet's destruction?
Does my heart leap for joy when I see kindness?
Does the snow on high peaks,
Phosphorescent under moonlight,
Still make me tremble with wonder?
Does God's beauty, in the Form of Christ,
Still make me sing?

Am I gathering dust?
Where is all the life that was in me?

It is all still there
as you love now
as you let yourself be loved now, by God, by your wife,
by others
as you seek out the stranger now
as you show tenderness
as you stand always against the loneliness
of the inconsolable heart

But so often I fall short—

Of course,
which is why Christ died for you

The wind in the mountains that I knew as a boy does
still
shake my heart:
When it soughs in pines, I quiver like a woman
at her lover's touch.
The solid matter of the world, its forms, lines, colours,
odours,
these do still thrill me unspeakably,
As does the unimaginable splendour
behind and underneath them;
Afternoon sunlight glorifying ivy on a city wall
still lifts my soul,
And the sea's stallions driving landward, manes flying,
still fill me with wild delight;
God's care, my wife's love, the goodness friends show
me,
these do still move me deeply;
A mother cradling her baby,
A father carrying his son on his shoulders,
A family parting at a railroad station,
A soldier being honoured for his courage—

        these sights do still make me weep.

Yet something in me sometimes stoops like Crete's old hills
    under the wear and tear of time and storm;
    And I have seen my foot trip, miss the next step,
    and my legs strain and falter and buckle;
    And sometimes sadness cloaks me like cloud enveloping
    high mountains,
    and I lose touch with those near me and feel fear;
    And at times in city streets, at the sight of all those young folk
    striding out, pushing history forward,
    I feel lost, left behind;
    And often I pass by some poor vagrant on a corner—
    someone *really* lost—
    and I feel nothing—I look away, I pass by, I go on.

Do I grow old?

Now I stroll dreaming through the Luxembourg Gardens
(I am alone this evening, unaccompanied by my wife)

and what I dream is the memory of strolling in those gardens
long ago
or of cycling as a boy to Montmartre one summer at dawn
and watching a beggar scavenge in rubbish bins
and a man hose down the cobblestones outside his café
and a young woman open her shutters and stare at the sky
while papers carrying news of what would never happen again
go spiralling down the narrow streets
in whirlpools of morning wind

Oh, it is not that I was especially happy then
(For most of us happiness is a discovery—
Even an invention—of memory,
Or an intimation of the ultimate fulfilment
Of a state of peace briefly experienced);
It is simply that more life lay ahead than behind
And prospects seemed numerous
So that the challenge of making choices
Eclipsed the sorrow of letting other choices not chosen
Subside into oblivion.

Perhaps that is what we mean by innocence

Nor is it that I now dwell in that past
As if it had been better than this present—
The issue is not really nostalgia,
And I have few illusions.
It is simply that the size of what is past
Now greatly outweighs the size of what lies ahead.
It is a quantitative matter
More than anything else
(Am I correct in saying this?).
What is past is past
And what is still to come in this life will also be past—
That is the problem in a nutshell,
That is the sorrow that dogs our days.

Is it not so, fellow traveller?

Experience and loss are inseparable companions.
The ever new, so quickly gone,
Cannot compensate its own swift passage,
Which seems to bear off into nothingness the person
one is,
So that, growing old, one's soul
Seems to wither like one's body

(I agree this is only appearance,
But the appearance is experienced as reality).
The happiness one may know in the present,
In giving and receiving love,
Is offset by the pain of its passing.
Successes or pleasures we might actually have tasted in the past,
Which, in imagination, we savour more keenly now
Than when we nearly had them,
Will never be ours to know,
And regret prowls like a wolf in the night.
The horizon of the past enlarges
As the future's perspective contracts.
We feel hemmed in by contrary pressures,
With all escape routes blocked, short of death.
Weaknesses of character, failures of will,
Hardhearted reactions to cries for love,
These are like arthritis in the bones
And trouble the mind insistently,
Which once, contemplating the extended future,
Was filled with great expectations.

It is not that joys are absent
Or satisfactions lacking—
But as energy flags and time shrinks,

One grows daily more conscious
Of loose ends one will never tie up,
Knowledge one will never have,
Beauty one will never see or see again,
Languages one will never speak,
Projects one will never realize—
Of all one might have done or seen or known
But failed to do or see or know, or could not,
Out of fear or incapacity or reality's constraints.

Companions of one's youth go forth into life and disappear,
The shared years fade like a dream;
Encounters with others come and go,
Like images flashed on a screen;
Friends one's own age suddenly have grandchildren,
One sees one's grey hair reflected in their eyes.

Then father and mother die,
Close ones are stricken,
Dear friends are buried in the ground—
One feels gutted,
Like a house where the furniture is carted off piece by piece.

The air grows cold,
One knows winter is coming

And so we must say this:
If forms perish into nothingness
And if the Void, not Form, is primordial;
If there is no forgiveness or hope of transformation
Into the fullness of the image of God,
Already in this life and in a Life to come;
And if one's own diminishing future holds out
No prospect of blessedness over the horizon
(As is the case for many,
Who have not perceived the eternity of Beauty Himself
Underneath and within
The manifold beautiful beings that come to be and pass),
Love must faint as meaning shrinks
And loneliness constricts the heart,
Until the past itself contracts and shrivels—
For without community
And the expectation of lasting communion between persons,
Time itself must die and become,
Like a tree without sap,
Dead wood.

But listen, dear one:
What was good and true and beautiful,
What was humble,
What in you implored and extended mercy,
Is stored in your heart,
In your heart that is like a seed
Containing all the nutrients needed for life,
Portending the eclosion in another soil,
In another life,
In a life of an immortal nature,
Of this seed that is your heart:
Under the pressure of grace,
The husk will break,
The chaff will fly off in the wind.

VI

From my storehouse rises now a memory
As the psaltery plays figures in the air
That ripple through the years
Like waves of energy through water,
And here I am again young,
Pulled by the tide of sheer vitality
Out from shore towards the open sea
Where winds blew fiercely and where,
So it seemed to me, the free man
Was the one who steered his barque
Solo in the gale, by force of will.

VII

Out on the path north, jauntily, I tramped,
    Bedroll, rifle, matches, backpack;
    I knew the trail well, I'd camped
    That way before, no need to worry,
    I'd be fine, the only thing I lacked
    Was a map, this was wilderness,
    No maps existed for a trek
Into these dark woods. *"You'll be sorry,"*
    Said a voice; I put it down to stress,
    Ignored it, tramped on into the gloom
Of spruce trees hung with beards of moss,
    Lightened by poplar and ghostly birch.
    In these wild parts, this world, no room
    For fear, I told myself. Be bold,
Trust your brains and instincts; no doom
    Befalls an honest man in search
    Of freedom. Truth be told,
    I was looking for the trapper's home,
    "Daganaw's cabin", the old
Pioneer from Scotland who'd come out

Around 1900 to roam
The north and trap. He settled down
In the wilderness alone,
A solitary man about
His business of trapping, far from town
Or ties to family or friend,
Making the woods and beasts his own
True love, lodestar of his life.
Few knew him. He grew into legend.
Where was his cabin? When did he die?
Who was Daganaw? I felt close to him somehow,
Though I was young;
I wanted to find out his end
And know the meaning of his life.

VIII

I ask myself a question:
Was that old pioneer an exile
Or a free man?
What was the nature of his solitude?
Perhaps his freedom was the fragment
Of a broken bowl,
Like the sea's echo in a conch shell
Pressed to the ear.
Listening to the shell,
You conjure the ocean,
But what you hear is not the ocean,
It is a memory of ocean evoked by a hum—
A *dream.*
And yet a real ocean does exist,
And neither the object of your dream
Nor the dream itself is an illusion.
Underneath and inside appearance is Reality.
Yet I ask: is not Invisible Reality itself—
For us who intuit it inside the Visible—
A kind of dream?
We come to be, pass, go hence;

Our encounter with the ocean comes to be, passes, goes hence;
The memory of our encounter with the ocean comes to be, passes,
goes hence.
It is the speaking of the thing that endures, the naming,
Provided the naming is not a taking possession—
This is how Invisible and Visible are joined.
The naming affirms relation,
And relation expresses love
And endures;
It is love that prompts the naming
And anchors in eternity
Bonds created now.

(So what was Daganaw's dream?
What bonds did he create?)

And I answer:
Yes, surely, what you say is true—
Yet so much of us goes unspoken, unnamed,
Even to those we love.

(Whom did Daganaw love?
Who loved him?)

So little of us is really shared—
Isn't that so?
Our words are like the waves of the sea,
Like the pleats on the surface of the ocean.
The rest of us goes unseen, unsaid—
Those great depths of water where myriad fish pass in the dark
And unknown currents cross.
No, you do not know who I am,
I do not know who you are;
You do not even know yourself who you are,
I do not even know myself who I am.

Yes. But we can know another more than you think,
We can know ourselves more than you suppose,
For we ourselves are known,
We are not lost:
Our Creator knows us and has always known us,
And God's Word has come into our midst.
If God did not know us and was not present in us,
We would be lost;
If Christ had not come and died and been raised up,
We would be lost;
If the Spirit of Holiness had not been poured into the world
To live within us and to fashion Christ's Body,

We would be lost;
If God had not made us in his image as spiritual beings,
Creatures gifted with speech,
Icons of the Word capable of giving and receiving love,
No communion with another would be possible,
We would be bodies imprisoned in skin;
And if, in Christ, God did not promise us eternity
(That transparent state of being-in-communion,
When we shall know him and others and ourselves
More fully and more fully and more fully),
And movement in time spoke only of loss
And not also of hope and renewal,
Love's horizon would be closed,
Love's fulfilment impossible,
Even love's tokens we've known would be tragic,
For ultimate meaning would be lacking,
Life would be defeated by death—
We would only know the aimless drift of tides,
The wash and repetition of waves,
The motion of great winds and waters circling the world,
Together with the ceaseless passing to and fro
Inside the darkness of the solitary self
Of unnamed myriad flitting fish.

IX

Foldedness, unfolding, infolding, dropping:
Bud's course,
Man's—
The sun's light brings life to flower,
Nor is it absent as the petals fall.
This is like the naming of a thing by the word,
The naming giving meaning,
An expression of love,
Not possessing but discovering,
Bringing into light what the thing is,
Defining it,
Establishing between the namer and the named
A bond,
So making sense of the existence
And the passing from existence
Of both namer and named,
Of their coming and their going hence.
And yet the naming of the thing,
The word we speak,
Is not the thing itself

But the apprehension of the experience of the thing.
They are two, but knotted—
It is their bondedness that counts,
That makes them what they are:
Two in one, one in two:
Foldedness, unfolding, infolding, dropping.

X

Christ with us here,
Christ with us now,
The Saviour and his saving work
Here and now,
With us, in us
Forever and now,
His Kingdom come

XI

Let us go now into isolation,
Into a place that is no place,
Whose denizens lack direction
And become like points on a graph without connection.
Here *present* shrinks to *instant*;
Past and future—present's parents—
Like castaways on ocean's emptiness,
Subside into indifferent darkness.
What we call *now* is orphaned,
Both form and hope are lost,
As when a vow is broken,
A covenant denied,
And infidelity unmoors the present
From both past and future,
So that the way ahead is lost like the way whence one came
And *all*—until meaning is given—becomes *same*
and is coated with ash.

XII

So (picking up the thread of my tale)
I left my father's house and tramped into wilderness.
The forest embraced me in its pleats,
Pine and spruce enfolded me.
Tree-trunks and branches
(And my own thoughts)
Were my company.
For hours I followed the faint trail northward,
Vestige of Daganaw's link with people.
Silence was a *basso continuo*.
Under the occasional whiff of wind
Solitude grew heavy like the colour green.
As I passed through clearings of poplar
dappled by sun-light,
The heart-shaped leaves consoled me.
But evergreen gloom soon descended again
As the trail wound away
Through the forest.

Where was I going?

Suddenly a covey of grouse flapped up from a tree;
I spun around, froze, gripped my gun;
The grouse flapped, squawked, flew off—
Stillness.
Leaves rustled somewhere
Wind
I wiped my brow.

I came to a fork.
Which trail to take?
A crooked pine marked the spot,
To the left a slope rising,
On the trees thick moss.
I chose the right fork.

Crooked pine, hill rising, beards of moss

Day waning.
I should be coming to a steep slope.
"When you reach a steep slope after many miles,"
An old-timer had told me,
"There's a path forks off up the hill to the east."
That slope at the last fork wasn't the one
He was talking about. It went west.

Are you sure that was west?
I came to a sharp turning.
The path veered left, keeping level.
To the right a steep slope.
I went on.
A faint track opened to the right, up the hill.
Yes.
East?
I *will*
I pressed up the hill.
Tree-limbs spikes moss-beards needles in my face.

Crooked pine, hill rising, beards of moss

"…forks off up the hill to the east."

I *will*

I pressed up the hill
Branches stabbed me
I was bleeding
Where's the trail?
Steep slope
It's the steep slope that counts
"…*to the east*"

Press on

I *will*

Press on to the top
Yes
Top
Yes
And there—
Daganaw's cabin!

The cabin lay below me in an overgrown clearing,
Its chimney like the stack of a steamship
Broken on rocks, the bulk of its broad-axed logs
Buried in the wild wrack of nettles and brambles,
Birch saplings, pines, vines, a riot of weeds.
The plank door, a tooth dangling;
The windows, vacant sockets;
The roof, a skull fractured by a fallen tree.
Ruin.
So it comes to this
I entered.
The smell of rats, mildew, rotting wood, decay.
Rusty cans, pans, crockery, a blackened skillet,
Chairs, table, a wood-box, a barrel stove,

Packrat-gutted bedding in a corner,
Snowshoes, kerosene lamp, a coffee pot,
Bowls, a cracked pail, jars, a tin tub,
A steamer trunk with travel stickers on it,
Steel traps, a leather halter, fire-tongs,
On one wall a bear-hide, legs splayed,
On another a photo of a couple on a city street
With words scrawled: *Iris, Edinburgh, 1898*;
And on a shelf beside it a wolf skull,
Fangs bared.

"You will die," I heard.
"Who are you?"
"Death."

"No."

Another voice said: "I am Daganaw who lived here."
And: "Those you love leave you,
You leave those you love.
They go out,
You go out,
No one returns.
There is incomprehension and grief.
You lose what you hope to possess.

Everything is taken away.
You are alone.
The law of life is loss,
Death."

"No."

Death said: *"You are lost."*

"No."

Outside where a garden had been once were trees,
Thick undergrowth,
Weeds.
In the dereliction I found a cross made of bars of iron,
Planted at the base of a pine.
On it was incised the name "Daganaw".
Who had planted it?

My bones lie here under sod,
White clouds drift above them.
My bones are white, fleshless.
My flesh has gone to worms,
My spirit to my Maker.
I am not here,

I am gone.
My bones remain,
But they are not me.
I have taken on a greater form,
I have been given Life,
I shall receive a spiritual body.
Do not pity my bones.

"Who were you?"
"I am Daganaw,
I have found mercy."
"How?"
"God found me."
"Did you love life?"
"Once, but I gave up."
"What do you mean?"
"I left it and died."
"How?"
"I despaired."
"Why?"
"The woman I loved left me.
It was my fault,
I wanted to possess her.
I fell into despair,
I turned in upon myself.

It is better not to love."

"Do you believe that?"

"Not now. But I believed it once,
I chose to believe it once."

"Why?"

"I cut myself off from others. I was lost, dead."

"You, a trapper, lost?"

"Yes. I fled. I gave up on life. I died."

"But you were free."

"No. I was trapped. I trapped myself."

"How?"

"I gave up hope. I said 'No' to life. It was my fault."

"But you could do what you wanted."

"No, that was an illusion.
What I really wanted to do—deep down—
I couldn't do. I couldn't love.
I wanted to love, but I couldn't.
I hated myself,
So I couldn't let the woman I loved be free.
I had an image in my mind,
I wanted her to be like the image.
So she left me.
She was right to go away, but it made me hate myself
even more.
I turned my back on men, on God—

I grew bitter and hard.
After that, I only wanted to be with trees and animals—
They accepted me,
They were kind to me,
Or indifferent.
They left me alone, which is what I thought I wanted.
And they couldn't answer back.
I hated myself."

"And that means you were lost?"

"Yes. If you don't love yourself, you're lost.
That's why I wanted to possess my woman,
To fill the emptiness in me.
I was afraid.
I was afraid of losing her, so I lost her.
I was afraid of loving.
I wanted my own way, though I hated myself—
I thought that was freedom.
I was proud, deluded—
Lost.
But God found me.
He used the animals and trees to show me I was acceptable,
To show me I was lovable.
That's how I came to myself.
God changed my heart."

Death said to me: *"You are lost.*
You want to find your way alone.
You will die."

"No."

Night was coming on.
I lay down to sleep by the pine-tree
Where the cross was planted.

I dreamed that a billion stars
Buried me deep in the earth.
They stood by my graveside
In white robes all night long,
Guarding me from the Void.
In the Void was chaos and ruin,
Violence and terror,
Solitary shapes never touching.
"This is hell," said the stars.
"Absolute loneliness.
It has invested the human heart
And God's creation."
But I lay at rest, protected,
Cradled in starlight and Original Peace.
The stars bore me on poles of silver

To the Tree of Life, which was a Man.
They gathered round the Man and worshiped.
Each star hung on the Tree as though
It were an apple on an Apple Tree.
I plucked an apple from the Apple Tree
That was a Man, and ate it.

I awoke.

I was lying in Daganaw's ruined garden
Under an overcast sky. No sun.
There stood the iron cross
With the carved name: "Daganaw".
Was this a dream too?

Who were you, Daganaw?
Who are you?

I heard his bones grumbling
Underneath the cross:
"We have been left behind,
Daganaw is gone,
He has found mercy.
As for us, we do not have the power of an endless life.
But Daganaw has been given the gift,

He is alive and will be raised."
How can this be?
"It will be on the Day when time itself is fulfilled."

Daganaw, where are you?
You say you were lost,
But your bones say you live.

And I heard the bones:
"Before he died, he opened himself to love,
To the love of the Son of God.
God the Father found him, he found the Father.
So he accepted himself as he was
And came out of hiding.
He accepted himself as the trees and animals accepted him,
As God accepted him—
He received himself as a gift from the hands of his Creator.
Then he asked God to forgive him his pride and self-hatred—
He chose life."

But how?

"He bowed his head and lifted up his heart in
thanksgiving
And worshiped."

Who lies here?
Who is under this cross?
How can it be that I hear these bones speak?

Is it I?
Is it I buried here
under loam and soft needles?

"No," said Death. *"You are lost."*

"No".

I heard the voice of Daganaw one last time:
"Choose life."

I fled.
I fled to the top of the hill
And crashed down the steep slope
I'd climbed the day before
Where was the path I'd turned from?
Farther south?

I veered left

Was this south?

Where was my compass?

I searched my pack

Nowhere

Gone

Lost

Fool!

Where was I?

I thrashed through the grey woods

No path

Maybe I'd gone too far south

Turn west

Was west right?

Maybe I've been going east

No

I bore right

West?

No sun

Right left south east west—

There was no right way

Crooked pine, hill rising, beards of moss

Everywhere were crooked pines hills rising beards of moss.

Suddenly I came on a trail
I lurched leftward
Southward?
Now a fork. Was this…?
No
It was flat here
No hill
It's not the trail I travelled yesterday
I chose the right fork, heading…
I searched the woods for signs
Recognizable signs
Familiar signs
Signs

Crooked pine, hill rising, beards of moss

Trees
Trees
Trees
Another fork
I chose the left branch
South?

East?
Where am I going?
I plunged ahead
Trees
A hill
Haven't I seen that big spruce before?
No
Where am I going?
Isn't that the crooked pine?
It must be
The land rises
It must be
I plunged ahead to the pine
No path
There's no path
No path
I'm turning in circles

I'm turning in circles

Where am I?
I don't know

I stopped, exhausted.
I was panting heavily.

I don't know where I am

"You are nowhere."

I'm in the wilderness alone

"You are nowhere."

Hills pines slopes hills pines poplar slopes hill pines slopes spruce hills

I'm lost

"You are lost," said Death.

"Yes."

Lost

I am lost

Ohgodohgodohgodohgodohgodlost

O GOD! GOD!

And that was when I heard the river,
A faint rushing sound away off,
The sound of water over rocks
Brought to my ears by a breeze.
The sound itself was not the breeze,
Nor leaves, nor wind brushing needles,
But the far-off faint exciting whisper
Of rapids, like the sound of a snare drum
Rustling in the high tops of the pines.

The river. The Nechako River. The river ran
East-West. It ran by the ranch three miles
To the west. From the ranch to the river
Was a trail I knew well, that came out
By the river where a great cedar stood.
If I followed the Nechako till I came
To the cedar, I'd find my way home.

"YES!"

And I lit out like a shot towards the water.

Going, filled with joy, exultant, I thought:
How did I stray so far from the path?

How could I have missed the trail?
How could I have swung so far to the west
When I thought I was heading northeast?

No answer, just the breeze in the pines, the poplars rustling,
the river far off.
It didn't matter. I was safe now. I'd found my way.
I lurched southwards, drunk on hope.
There was no path to follow, it didn't matter.
The river led me on in the depths of the forest, humming.

"Oh, do not ask about love, my friend,
You'll know what it is when it finds you.
You can only keep what you're given, my friend,
What you strive to possess will escape you.
Don't ask what it's like to be lost, my friend,
You'll know what it's like when you're found."

At last I reached the river, the lovely Nechako.
The sun, loosed from clouds, gleamed on the water
Like quartz-flecks in granite, while the blue tide
Moved between the banks like an ambling bear.
Above where the rapids were singing their song,

I stripped off my clothes and plunged in.
The river swallowed me whole.
I swam to mid-stream and back, stroking strongly.
My father's ranch was close—ten miles, twenty?
No matter. It was close. I was *free*.

A flock of wild geese flew over my head,
Winging southeast. They honked, I waved. They honked
Again, wings beating. "*Go, great geese,*" I cried. "*So long!*"
Then I dressed, grabbed my pack, took my canteen and gun,
And followed the wild geese east towards home.

XIII

Voices are calling me to worship:
"Join us on the ladder to heaven,
The ladder of prayer,
Jacob's ladder,
The ladder of Bethel,
Where the Sovereign Lord descends and ascends,
The Lord who meets us,
Who creates and saves us,
Lord of earth and sky,
Of all things past, present, future:
In our communion he takes pleasure."

XIX

The psaltery strikes soft chords,
Conjuring dreams;
Reflections on memory's pond
Shimmer in moonlight;
Ripples run over the water,
Bearing backward the heart
To days gone, forward
To times yet to be
And to God, our Life,
Source and End of our longing.
The soul's growth over years
Gives sense to events
Experienced unreflectively
Once upon a time.
The weight of days on days
Distills meaning,
Transmutes sediments,
So making gems in old rock.
Under the psaltery's soft incantations
The pure jewels sparkle in light;

Truth, gleaming brightly,
Shines with God's Beauty,
Rejoicing the senses;
The heart, buoyant,
Flushed with new hope,
Soars high on love's fugue
Playing through time.

THE TRINITY SUITES

SUITE I : CREATION MARRED

Suite I.1. The Lamb

I was a boy. It was long ago. It was yesterday.

I burst out from the log cabin
Where my father and I and a hired hand
Lived in a space made of cubicles and a kitchen
With a barrel stove for heating
And a wood stove for cooking
And a table for eating
And a sink for washing
And a few chairs for sitting
And nails for hanging things
And shelves for piling things
And a kerosene lamp
And a wood-box
And pails of water
And a bearskin nailed to one wall.

I burst out into day,
My boy's heart full of wild birds,
The air a heron poised on one leg,
The sky a robin's egg,
The girdling forest a wreath.
Oh—*day!*

I breach morning like a calf bucking,
I buck across the oat-field to the woods,
I fall out of blue into green,
The forest enfolds me like a father,
I sink into spruce shade.

I lope,
I lope over brown mats of needles,
I breathe pine-spice,
I lope.
Chanting birds fill my ears—
A choir!
Joy!
Sun breathes in the green boughs,
Sun kisses the brown trunks,
Gold melts among the shadows of the forest floor.

At the edge of the woods the path gave onto the
meadow
Where my father's flock of sheep had been grazing.

and there a hump a white hump
a lamb
a lamb lying there
a lamb on the ground facing me
belly open
slashed
the whole length of the belly slashed open
a coyote did it
the guts of the lamb on the grass
spilled out on the grass
bowels
the stomach sits like a balloon on the grass
it sits outside the emptied belly on the bloody grass in a
pool of blood
the legs are splayed
stiff like sticks
the wool round the belly is red
red white wool
bloody white wool of a lamb—
And oh the head!
poor little sweet head!

pink nose ears
oh poor little sweet head!
eyes wide dark stones staring empty no life no life
oh poor little sweet head!
poor little sweet head
dark stones
dead
oh!
My God! My God!

Suite I. 2. The Howl

Out beyond the hayfield
Where field and forest meet,
Wild country stretches to the sea.
Evergreen clothes the land
Like a bear's coat: dense,
Thick, dark. The yellow sun,
Sliding down the sky
Above the trackless wild,
Barely penetrates the green.
The forest is a form of night,
Solid as a shadow
Bolted to the back of earth.
Under the eyes of stern pines,
Noble spruce, resolute fir,
Occasional copses of poplar,
Wild creatures live and move
And have their animal being
Among windfall, fern, moss, roots.
Here moose crash, deer bound,
Birds flit, bears lumber by,

Wolves and coyotes prowl and howl.

I too howl. Clinging to the cattle chute
Inside the log corral,
I lift my eyes to the stars
That beckon me while night
Comes upon the world, and howl.
A feather of moon floats
On the black lake above my head,
As my howls go echoing
Across the meadows to the forest.

And I hear a wolf's howl
Echoing back from the edge of the woods
Where the trees hunker down
For the planet's turn through night,
A plaintive cry
(Is he mimicking mine?)
Carrying the longing of creatures
From the gravity of earth
To the listening ears of heaven,
The comfort-bearing stars.

Suite I.3. Loss

I shall go away now
I shall leave.
My shirt of many colours will be shredded
I shall leave my father and my stepmother
I shall leave coyotes, cattle, dung,
The clear creek bubbling through the meadow,
Wildness,
The North.

I shall go into exile.
I shall go to the city and walk on pavement.

I won't ride bareback through the forest again.
In my memory I'll hear the wind soughing in pines,
I'll smell the clover,
The wild strawberries will taste sweet in my memory.

I shall go away now,
I shall leave my father.

Oh, my shirt will be sewed back together again

With strips of culture;
Grace will make of it a wearable patchwork.
I'll manage to be presentable in acceptable society
And acceptable in unpresentable society.
Grace will enable that, not I:
Neither poetry nor metaphysics nor differential equations;
Not the study of medicine or law or political science;
Neither archaeology nor geology,
Neither history nor theology;
Not literature,
Not art,
Not even music—
Only *grace*.

I shall be a wanderer,
Discovering here and there,
Now and then,
Plots of wildness,
Where air and water and earth and fire
Are air and water and earth and fire.
Like Dante remembering Tuscany
Even in the heart of the heavenly embrace,
I shall ache always and forever
Remembering my Eden,
The Little Creek Ranch in British Columbia:

The mud-caked jeep,
The manure pile,
The hay-shed stacked with bales;
My stepmother showing me how to make pies
And find mushrooms in the woods after rain;
My father teaching me to wield an axe,
Milk a cow,
Drive a tractor.
My father called me 'son'.
He was always happy to be with me.
He said he was grateful to have a son.
I was proud.

And when I boarded the plane the last time sixty years ago,
And at all our partings since then until the last,
My father always waved his right arm
In a wide arc back and forth,
Back and forth,
Until I lost sight of him,
Until I lost *him*.

I shall go away now.
I shall drop into the world.
I shall try to find the moon above the streetlamps.
Neither the wolf's howl nor the loon's cry

Will wake me in the night.
No.
It will be the pulse of sirens,
The ululation of ambulances and fire engines,
The moan of police vans:
These will break over my sleep like waves,
They will tear me from slumber.
I will never take the pine-needled path into the woods again,
Or drink earth's smells and silence.
No.
I'll wriggle in a skein of noisome streets
Like a fly in a web.

Exile

The sprinkled stars once were sparks from heaven's fire
That glowed in the night as I blew on them;
Now they're man-made images on photographs and screens
Picturing by electronic contrivance
Glorious entities that the multitudes in cities
Never lay eyes on.

I shall join those multitudes.
I shall not stand again under the enormous night,

To be nourished by beauty
And the truth it radiates;
No, I shall survive on digital mediations,
Virtual galaxies abstracted from space
And delivered to my cell on screens.
Deep space in its glory
Will unfold at a finger's touch—
And, yes, I shall rejoice at the wonders revealed—
But rarely again shall the jeweled vault of heaven
Be itself the object of my awe.

Oh, loss!

And now look:
The curtain falls, the lights go on.
Loud clapping.
Then the curtain rises again.
What we see now is just a stage.
The actors come from the wings and take a bow.
They are themselves again, people like you and me.
You are disoriented.
(Perhaps you are disoriented as you read this.)
You applaud the actors vigorously,
But in your mind the characters they played
Still stride across the set, compressing life
Into a small square space and three hours.

The play had transformed stone to gems;
The commonplace had become precious;
The daily, turned inside out,
Had displayed its timeless lining;
The prosaic had become a poem.

Now you rise from your seat,
Join the bustling crowd,
And walk out into the city.
You are back in normal time and space,
Subject to their constraints.
Underneath your excitement
You feel depressed.
You try to make sense of your emotion.
What is real?
Where is home?
Something has been lost.
What?
You feel like a waif.

Yet the freedom you knew for three hours—
The absorption into a world outside yourself
That you did not invent, that was a gift—
Is not lost. It is held in trust. Its memory
Is an image of the reality it prefigures,
When what you will have lost, will be loss itself,

When what you will have found, will be Life.
Death will have died.

How can this be?

Loss itself revealed this truth to me.

"So long, son," said my father.
We were standing on the tarmac near the plane.
"I believe in you," he said.
Then he hugged me in his strong arms.
My stepmother kissed me.
I boarded the plane,
Which was a tomb.
As it lifted from the ground,
I saw my father on the runway waving.
His right arm made a wide arc back and forth,
Back and forth.
He waved and waved,
He grew smaller,
Then he was gone.
A cloud buried the plane.

For hours I wept.
For hundreds of miles
I cried and cried.

Life had been ripped from me.
My happiness was frozen,
Like the figures on Keats's Grecian urn.
My many-coloured shirt was shredded.
I was orphaned.

Henceforth I would walk on pavement,
Sirens would wail inside my dreams.

Exile

Yet once my tears were spent,
Once I had come to the end of myself,
Once the grief for my mortality was wrung out like a rag,
Somehow it was given me to know
It was not so,
That the figures on my urn would move again,
That life would flow again into those mortal scenes,
That I'd come home again one day.

Oh—a deer bounds in my heart!
Water riffles in the creek
Frogs plop
I'm galloping on Paint bareback in the meadow
Sparks from heaven's fire flash in the night

Joy!

Thus did loss somehow sow in me hope's seed.

Grace

And yet—oh, loss!
O great loss!
Years later I still tremble,
Remembering.
Remembering:
"So long, son."

But I am grateful,
I shall always be grateful.
My father was grateful to have a son,
I was grateful to have a father.

My face is turned toward the stars.

Suite I.4. The Barracks

Pressed on the sulphurous horizon like centipedes
Squashed on a mouldy wall, looping causeways
Span the watercourses binding skeins
Of reticulate structures on the marshland,
Cubes of pipes and tubes and brick stacks
Belching gas-flares and roiling smoke-plumes,
Hell's attendants at the court of oil
Celebrating the ruination of the planet.

On a military complex farther inland,
A stone's throw from the consumptive wasteland,
Two pathetic structures face each other:
A dilapidated barracks slated for destruction,
And a shed for the maintenance of army vehicles
And the repair of military equipment.
The buildings stand mired in perpetual mud
On a broad plain dotted with similar structures
And buffeted by fierce winds from the north.

Between the buildings no converse is imaginable.
The barracks houses soldiers being mustered
Out of the army, for reasons of collapsed health
Or mental handicap, men who have shown themselves
Unfit for the rigours of military life.
The shed is occupied by expert mechanics,
Personnel skilled in the repair of machines.

Beside the buildings is a nondescript shrub,
Alone of its kind on the destitute plain
And mired in mud like the barracks and shed.
All winter long it shivers in cold, and icicles
Sprout on its branches like glittering twigs.

An inmate of the barracks, ill and downcast—
Assigned, until discharge, the important task
Of sweeping daily the decrepit building—
Walked out one April morning when the snow
Was melting and mud lay ankle-deep,
And discovered a miracle:
The frail shrub was laden with yellow blooms!
At the sight of organic life and the display of colour,
His heart leapt up. Ignorant in botany,
He thought to inquire of one of the personnel
In the maintenance shed (where much noisy

Activity was going on this April morning)
What might be the name of the flowering bush.

He approached the shed, where a mixture of grease,
Gas, oil, and mud made a moat of filthy slush.
A huge man built like a refrigerator
Stood just outside the open door,
Hammering the twisted fender of a jeep.
"Sorry to bother you," the barracks inmate greeted him.
"I wonder if you could help me?"
The hammering stopped. "Yeh?"
"Snow's melting, eh? Good sign. Been a long winter."
Silence.
"I noticed this bush here. Yellow blossoms. Real pretty.
Kind of unexpected in these parts."
Silence.
"I was wondering, do you happen to know the name of
it—
The bush, I mean?"
The giant gasped and turned purple;
For a moment he just stared;
Then he exploded like an artillery shell.
"What!" he shouted, waving his arms wildly.
"What the–"
In a rage he advanced towards the man

Who had asked the unlikely question.
"You want to know the name of a goddamn bush?"
He brandished his hammer, trembling with fury.
"…a goddamn bush!"
The other retreated, terrified.
The giant kept coming.
Then the inmate of the barracks turned
And ran for dear life towards the house.
Behind him he heard a crazy laugh.
At the door, breathing hard,
He looked back and saw the giant surrounded
By the maintenance personnel,
All of them laughing uproariously.
"Now I get it!" the huge man cried, gesticulating triumphantly.
"I get it!"
And a final shout, jubilant:
"You're one of the *crazies*!"

Suite I.5. The River of Rubbish

I

An imagined utopia we escape to,
Set, say, on a Caribbean island,
Reveals the precariousness
Of speculation on ideal reality
In any setting subject to the vagaries
Of natural phenomena or the miseries
Occasioned by spiritual corruption.

In an imagined utopian city,
Sewage, rubbish, trash of all kinds
Would be disposed of with planned efficiency;
Sewers, dumps, methods for recycling
Would impose upon human waste and detritus
An order preserving health and well-being;

But in an utopia undermined by avarice,
By fear, exploitation, and the use of violence
And occult practices to achieve one's ends,

Refuse is likely to pile up in the city streets
(Infrastructure will not have been built or maintained),
And garbage will accumulate on the canal
embankments.

II

On a beach west of the island's chief city,
Where palm trees sing in the clear air
And the sea is the hue of forget-me-nots
And the sand underfoot is soft
And coloured gold like Byzantine icons,
A couple came to bathe one summer afternoon,
Expecting an experience of perfection.

For two days diluvial rain had been pounding
The utopian city thirty miles to the east,
Flooding the streets and sweeping the refuse
Down to the putrid canals and out to the ocean.
Currents and winds had carried the tons of debris
Westward, creating a river of rubbish

Along the coast, twenty yards wide and forty
Miles long, a colourful ribbon winding
Like a tapeworm in the ocean's intestines:

Chairs and tires, mattresses, wheel rims, boxes,
Tins, cans, bottles, plastic bags, wire, cables,
Electronic devices, rotting garbage.

The couple expecting perfection stared in horror,
Watching the ribbon undulate offshore like a snake,
While the floating debris, borne by the waves,
Polluted the golden sand of Byzantium.
The leaning palms waved their fronds sadly
And keened in the afternoon wind.

That night the cavernous heavens wept,
The stars turned to tears.

SUITE II : HUMANITY GROANING

Suite II.1. Transgression

I

We're in fallen time now,
At a point where son and father clash.
It has been and must be so until the end,
The end that will inaugurate another time,
A time when self-possession will be in God fully,
Hostility will give way to peace,
Competitive striving will cease,
Condemnation will have gone down over the edge
Of the old world into the abyss,
Love will have taken up becoming into being.

But now we're in old time still,
Repeating a primordial pattern that requires redemption.
The space we are crossing is primeval,
Befitting the event.
This is wilderness:
Not the earlier wilderness but another,

No less wild,
No less vast:
Matted forest reaching to horizons hung on air,
Jeweled lakes like peacock eyes,
Streams like veins in anatomical drawings.

II

On a windless day once,
In the silence of a hot afternoon,
As the earth turned slowly
And the sun slid down the empty sky,
Four men looking no larger than bugs
On the broad canvas of wilderness
Were paddling in wooden canoes
On a small vein of the spacious land.
My father and I were paired in one canoe,
He stern, I bow;
A young friend and our guide were paired in the other.
We are gliding on the slow current between banks of spruce,
Watching, listening, all senses alert.
The gurgle of paddles in water,
The knock of wood on gunnels,
The wing-flap of startled birds:

No sounds but these stir the silence.

A time passes,
We paddle,
The sun slides lower.
Then abruptly in a river-bend our guide lifts his paddle:
"Rapids ahead."
We grow tense and strain our ears—
On the air comes the susurrus of waters.
"Remember to aim for the Vs," I caution my father.
"It's the only way to stay shy of the rocks."
The lead canoe quickens its pace,
The current flows swiftly.
We can see the chop now;
The banks close in;
The noise grows loud, drums rumbling.
We're hitting riffles, bouncing;
Waves slap our bow;
The water churns around us,
To port foaming over stones,
To starboard rolling in sheets over round rocks.
I glimpse the first canoe ahead of us bucking;
We're in wild water now,
We toss, pitch.
I stroke desperately to avoid a big rock.

"The V," I yell at my father. "Steer left!"
Unaccountably my father steers right.
"Watch out!"
The bow knocks the boulder broadside.
"You're crazy!" I cry. "What the—?"
Now the canoe is scraping on stones.
"Steer left, dammit! We're running aground!"
I push against the stones with all my strength,
Then paddle frantically.
The canoe careens into the deeper channel,
The current sweeps it over sunken rocks.
We manage to slip through a broad V between shoals,
Then we're flushed out into calmer waters.
The hiss of the rapids fades behind us;
The other canoe is thirty yards ahead, coasting.
Quiet comes over the river.
I think: "We made it."

But my heart is not quiet.
In the turmoil I had shouted disrespectfully at my father;
I had dishonoured him.
I felt sick, but said nothing.

"Well, we made it," I mutter finally, not turning around.
No answer.

"We almost didn't."
Silence.

My father had stopped paddling.
The only sound to be heard
In the empty wilderness
Was water lapping on the sides of the canoe.

III

Christ met me on a dark night eight years later.
He came into the wilderness of my soul
And took his seat in the stern of my canoe.
He gave me grace to ask forgiveness of my sin.
I went to see my father soon after.
"Do you remember the time I swore at you
On our canoe trip?" I asked him.
"When we were caught in the rapids?"
His expression grew troubled.
"Yes, son, I remember it well."
"I want to ask you to forgive me, please.
I know we were in danger, but that's no excuse.
I yelled at you, I was disrespectful.
I'm really sorry."
My father's face brightened like a landscape

When sunlight breaks from behind dark clouds.
"Of course I forgive you, son," he said.
He wrapped his arms around me,
I wrapped my arms around him.
Tears rolled down my cheeks.
"This is the happiest day of my life," he exclaimed.
"And mine," I rejoined.

The air was full of laughter.

Suite II.2. Rats

Six rats swam across the Hudson to the shore
Of Manhattan, to take up residence in sewers
And derelict squats, like the rats that feasted on corpses
In the trenches of France a century past, beasts
Happy in squalor, that breed in the slums of cities
And join their human cousins to feed on death.

These scampering creatures grow fat on death.
They clamber from the river on New York's shore
To invest the wretched squats in the great city's
Squalid precincts and prowl the sewers,
Where muck and gungy offal are gulped by the beasts
Hungrily—Ah, such fare rivals the corpses!

All roads through the ages are lined with corpses;
In our memory's hold they stink of rabid death.
On Tamerlane's pyramids of skulls, beasts
Scuttled and chewed, like the rats from the Jersey shore
And the fat-rats that sit at desks in high-rise sewers
And oppress the hoi-polloi in teeming cities.

Varieties of rats inhabit cities.
Mafioso fill the bloody streets with corpses;
Sex-lords and pimps fill their pockets with death;
Addicts crouch in alleys or retreat to sewers
Like the rats that scramble up Manhattan's shore,
Victims turned by dealers into avid beasts.

Six rats swim over from New Jersey, beasts
Like the billion other rats that live in cities.
A-crawl with lice, they scamper up the shore
And nose their way to tenements where corpses
Stick their arms with needles, grin at death,
Then float on highs through aromatic sewers.

Can anything but rats survive in sewers?
Supposing God came down to love the beasts
Whose sordid lives are caricatures of death?
He knows the hearts of those who live in cities.
"Come to me!" he cries. "Turn from the corpses
You've become, buried on death's stinking shore!"

Our dwellings need not be the fetid cities
We've constructed, inhabited by corpses.
We're called to live in joy, on heaven's shore.

Suite II.3. The Mop

Oh, such unnameable sorrow,
That one should choose to plunge into night!
That one should fear less the yawning blackness
Than our world's unbearable plight!

I stood on the embankment by the River Seine,
Beside an old barge moored with a rope.
A mop up-river caught my roving eye,
A bundle bobbing in the current.

The day was bright, the sky pale blue,
The air sweet with scents of summer.
Sycamores lined the quiet quayside,
Flower beds painted the grass.

I watched the mop as it drew near the barge,
Its coarse yarn rising and falling—
And then I saw it was no mop at all,
But a head of gray hair on a corpse.

The corpse came floating straight up in the water,
A middle-aged woman, well-dressed;
It came between the barge and the riverbank—
I nearly touched the hair with my hand.

The woman's water-logged face was livid,
Her brow wrinkled, cheeks puffed up;
The lids on her sunken eyes were closed
Like the shutters on an empty house.

The corpse made its way through the channel
Between the barge and the bank of the river;
Its posture was stately, arms lifted slightly,
The matted hair wafting in the current.

I mused a long while on the riverbank
Until the mop disappeared out of sight;
The dead woman settled in my memory
While her corpse floated off down the Seine.

None will ever know the woman's sorrow,
The despair that drove her to jump.
May the Lord Christ raise her to eternal Life
When he comes to redeem our world!

Suite II.4. The Traffic Island

I

No one would have guessed that the hirsute man
With the rheumy eyes had been an executive once
In a large corporation with affiliates in twelve countries,
Who had spent twenty-five years flying business class
around the world,
Going from city to city, airport to airport, hotel to hotel,
Attending high-level meetings with important
executives during the day
And sleeping at night by himself in single hotel rooms
With only TV for company.

One would not have guessed that this unshaven man in
the soiled brown coat,
Sprawled on a bench on a traffic island in the middle of
Broadway and Ninety-Third Street, New York City,
Swilling cheap wine with two other sodden companions,
Oblivious to the honking cars and trucks and indifferent
pedestrians—

One would not have guessed that this man with dirty sneakers
Had once pulled down a large salary and owned two houses,
Had a wife who left him because he was always away travelling,
And two sons who grew up hardly knowing their father
And who zigzagged through life looking for the masculine love
They never had and finally threw their father out of the house
When he took to drink and gambled away the family money.
One would not have guessed any of these things, observing
The unkempt figure on the traffic island in the middle of Broadway.

Nor would the man himself in the brown soiled coat
Have guessed that he was God's creation,
Made in God's image and much beloved of his Maker,
Who had known him even before the earth was formed,
The great deeps poured out, the mountains piled up,
Before plants and dense forests covered the rock with green,
Before animate creatures emerged out of molecules—

Swimming, crawling, creeping, swarming, running—
Creatures patiently fashioned by Him who calls beings
out of nothing,
The Maker who sent His Word to call the hirsute man to
himself
So that he would know his true identity and receive his
true name
And no longer be lost and ceaselessly voyaging,
Ceaselessly striving,
Dying—
So that he would know he was beloved of his Creator
And welcome,
If he chose to hear God's call,
To share the Father's joy.

The hirsute man would not have guessed any of this.
Oh, perhaps he'd heard about it once,
Sort of,
Once when he was young,
But that would have been a long time ago,
A very long time ago.

Oh sorrow, sorrow!

O Father, I cry to you, have mercy!
Lord, have mercy!

II

No, the hirsute man would not have guessed any of this.
Nor would the lizard-like figure with the corrugated face
Who sat hunched beside him on the bench chain-smoking
And swigging jerkily from a bottle wrapped in brown paper.
In days gone by he rode the rails across America's plains,
Worked on oil-rigs in Texas,
Herded cattle in Colorado,
Felled trees in Oregon,
Cut roads in Utah.
In the valleys of California he picked grapes,
On the prairies of Montana he stacked hay,
In the mountains of Idaho he fought fires.
The man rode space,
The horizon was his home.
It was said he once had a woman in Boise,
Another in Santa Fe:
No one knows, it was long ago.
It was also said he killed a man in Butte, Montana,
And did time in jail:

No one knows, it was long ago.

The man once was quick as a ferret,
Tough as a goat,
With bright eyes and a nose like a blade;
Now his grizzled face was a rockslide.
No one ever told him he was loved—
So he kept moving,
He kept on moving.
No one ever told him the Son of God
Had come amongst us and suffered like a thief
So that vagabonds who scoured the earth
To fill up broken hearts and off-load guilt
Could be rooted in heaven and find peace.
He never walked with Jesus through Galilee,
He never saw love set people free,
No hand ever caressed his face,
Nor eyes told him he was wonderful.
So he looked to himself to find freedom,
Space was his lover.
He used to think:
"If I can just keep moving,
I'll be free."
So he kept moving.

Well, there's nowhere left for him to move now,
He's at the end of the line,
Space has run out,
There's nowhere left for him to go now.
On the traffic island where he sits all day,
The only move he makes is to light his smokes
And swig from the bottle in the brown paper bag.
Occasionally he dreams he's riding the rails
somewhere under an enormous sky,
Somewhere in Texas, Arizona, Wyoming, Utah,
But then he wakes up and finds himself on a traffic island
In the middle of Broadway and Ninety-Third, New York City,
With trucks and cars going by him on both sides, honking loudly,
And passers-by eyeing him with cold indifference.

Heavenly Father, receive this poor man!
Have mercy!
Christ, have mercy!

III

Looking at the third member of the trio on the bench
On the traffic island on Broadway and Ninety-Third Street,
One could never have imagined that once upon a time
He had been a structural engineer in total control of his life—
Career, wife, children, God—
And in total ignorance of his own heart,
With the result that one spring night in Central Park,
At a production of *Antony and Cleopatra*,
He fell in love with the actress playing Cleopatra
And experienced a total meltdown.
He abandoned his family to pursue the beautiful actress,
He dropped his career to pursue the beautiful actress,
He gave up his whole life for the beautiful actress,
Not for one moment suspecting all the while
That his father's abuse of him when he was a child
Had set him up for an identity crisis in later years.
Looking for the person he was,
He became another person than the person he was.
His wife divorced him and remarried,
His children refused to have anything to do with him,
The beautiful actress soon tired of him
And traded him in for a new model—
Whereupon he lost his mind,

The same keen instrument that once had everything
under control
And that used to calculate the load-bearing potential of
I-beams.

He had just enough reason and money left
To be able to rent a tiny room in a run-down building
On Broadway and Ninety-Eighth Street.
When the weather was good he sat alone in the park
Or joined his colleagues on the traffic island on Ninety-
Third Street.
Children stared at his bright yellow jacket and green
pants
Held up with suspenders.
He doffed his top-hat and blew kisses at them,
The way he used to do for the beautiful actress.
With his slender fingers he played scales on the air
And conducted imaginary choirs.
The pigeons flocked to the island when he was there;
Sometimes they hopped on his shoulders
And plucked bread from the rim of his hat.

This enigmatic figure in the bright yellow jacket
Could not have imagined that Jesus came to give him
back himself.

He had no idea that God was the Father who had sent the Son
So that fractured souls like him could be restored
And know themselves to be adopted sons of the Most High God,
Through the work of the Great Prince, Christ.
If the Word of the Most High God had been spoken,
His Breath could have breathed on the broken heart of this child
And repaired it. God's Wind blowing through the cold Void
Could have stood the man on his feet and made him whole.

But the Word had not been spoken,
At least not in any way that he could hear it.
So the past had hardened into rock,
The present was a fantasy,
The future did not exist.
For the man who once had been an engineer,
Only mercy could avail.

O Father, have mercy!
Hear my mute cries!
Lord Jesus, have mercy!

Suite II.5. You'll be Safe There

I

We were like cockroaches scuttling every which way
When a light goes on in the kitchen in the middle of the night.
We were cockroaches from all over Gikongoro.
"Go to the Technical School on the hilltop,"
The local mayor broadcast.
"You'll be safe there."
The mayor was a big man in the region,
Surely we could trust him.
So we came to Murambi from all over Gikongoro,
Thousands of us Tutsis every day for a week.
We took refuge in the classrooms of the Technical School,
Dozens of buildings like barracks spread across the hilltop.
"You'll be safe in the school," the mayor had said.
"They don't attack schools."
Most of us didn't believe him,

But what choice did we have?
He was an important person, after all,
He had authority.
To stay in our houses was suicide,
And we couldn't all hide in the banana groves.
We had no choice.
Packed together like merchandise in containers
We ate the little food we had
And waited in terror.
The *Interahamwe* began to arrive one night in the second week.
Hundreds took up positions around the hill,
Circling it like a noose.
They kept at a distance from the classrooms
And lay low among the trees and bushes fringing the hill.
At night we could see their fires.
They were like wind that rises when clouds cover the sun;
They were like poison gas spreading invisibly in the air.
One could reach out a hand and touch our fear.
The killers knew we would soon go hungry,
So they bided their time.
They were afraid too.
Cockroaches are frightening, after all;

They *infest* places.
The numbers of the militia increased every night.
Some of us said, "They're not going to attack us,
They're just trying to scare us,
They wouldn't attack a school."
We reminded ourselves of what the mayor had said.
The mayor, after all, had urged us to take refuge in the school.
He'd assured us we'd be safe there.
He was an important official—
Surely he could be trusted,
Surely he wouldn't betray us.

II

Up from some subterranean realm,
From some huge cave
Lodged in the bowels of the world,
Some vast hollow cavern
Where bats flit and peep
And thick worms wriggle on the stone floor
And hang writhing from the high roof,
Seeps **Black**.
An effluvium.
Through fissures in the rock

> ***Black** seeps up,*
> *Seeps.*
> *It invades the world's surface,*
> *Settles like soot,*
> *Coils like fumes from smokestacks,*
> *Coats like pitch.*
> ***Black.***
> *And where it seeps, settles, coils, coats,*
> *It turns white;*
> *Then it congeals and is impermeable;*
> *It becomes a crust caking the heart,*
> *Numbing reason.*
> *It suffocates conscience.*

III

The *Interahamwe* attacked at dawn on the fourth day.
Hundreds of drug-crazed Hutus swarmed across the hilltop
And broke down the doors of the classrooms
Where we were lined up like cigars in boxes.
They cut us down with machetes,
Swiping, slashing.
We flailed our arms wildly to defend ourselves:
The men tried to protect the women,

The women tried to protect the children.
The air was full of shrieks, howls, moans.
There were grunts, thumps, thuds.
Blood was everywhere.

Red, red

They cut us down;
Then they moved on to the next house.

IV

I lay buried half-dead under bodies piled ten deep.
I was not really conscious.
"God!" my heart cried in the void. "*Father!*"

And then before my eyes rose up a vision of the crucified Jesus
Hanging on the wooden cross.
His arms welcomed me,
His hands nailed to the cross-bar gathered me to himself.
His eyes looked with infinite love on our mutilated bodies.

The cross stood high on the hilltop of Murambi.
It was Night.
As I was looking, suddenly there was *Light*.
The Light burst forth,
It became like the blaze of ten suns,
It engulfed the Night.
And then I saw the Lord Christ rise from the cross—
Like a sail filling with wind,
He rose!

Embarkation!

Rising behind him,
Surging into glory,
Multitudes attended him—

Oh, companions!
Dear companions!
Sisters! Brothers!

Numberless as the sand grains on the world's beaches,
As the leaves on the world's trees,
Myriads rose in his train:
I saw them streaming into Light—
Life!

And I heard a Voice boom like the sound of great waters:
"The Lie has been cast out!"

We dead *live!*

SUITE III : EARTH REDEEMED

Suite III.1. You Shall Cherish Her

Love settled on the smile across the room
And said: This is she. You shall cherish her
All your years: her radiance today,
Her beauty in the middle passage, her loveliness
In age. She is yours to keep and hold.
Her smile is like a leaf in morning sun,
Her laughter like water burbling over stones;
Her heart is glass, transparent; her will
A compass, fixed to do the bidding of her Lord.
Cherish her, she is woman, she is yours.
You must endure the strain of time. Each trial
Will be occasion for your love to grow.
This woman is my gift, says God. Take her as wife.
In her beauty lies the mirror of eternal life.

Suite III.2. New People

We were new people,
We were all kinds of people
Tumbling out of incoherent lives
Into God's huge Hand.

We were so many fish,
We were all kinds of fish
Pulled out of streams and lakes and ocean depths
And caught up in Christ's Net.

We were myriads from all over,
We were multitudes from everywhere,
Plucked from city, nation, the whole world
And assembled in one Body.

We were a messy lot,
A sundry lot, heterogeneous,
Invited by Love to consent to be loved
And embrace Love's Life.

We were young and old,
We were black, white, brown,
We were rich and poor and everything between,
All gathered in one Spirit.

Some of us were bad news,
Some were like you, dear reader,
But all were lonely and lost and aching somewhere,
And humble enough to admit it.

A local group met to pray,
We met together to talk to God.
He spoke to us about the Way of Love,
He taught us the disciplines of Truth.

He forgave us our sins,
Washed away our guilt,
Scraped the crust off our souls.
He gave us eyes to see all things new.

We broke bread with him at his table,
He broke bread with us at ours;
He surrendered his life, we surrendered ours,
Each was a gift to the other.

We worshipped Christ in one Spirit,
We glorified God the Father;
The joy of the Lord was our strength,
His risen life was our hope.

"Christ is risen!" we sang.
"The Lord has ascended on high!"
"He will come again!" we sang.
"Death won't have the last word."

We were grateful people,
A people making new beginnings.
We were clay being modeled in his image,
Sculptures being fashioned for his service.

We came from all over, a messy lot,
But God bound us tightly together;
He sent us on our way towards the heavenly Gates,
His Spirit filled our hearts with joy.

Suite III.3. The River of Life

Summer plied the air with heat.
The Cirque de Montvalent,
By the iron bridge near Gluges,
Threw wide its limestone arms to greet us.
The sun sizzled like an egg in a pan.
Bathers, heads like balloons, bobbed
In the purling current of the Dordogne River.
The grizzled cliff facing us, cave-riddled,
Its top fringed with stunted oaks,
Squinted at us out of hollow sockets.

My beloved and I, she a viola,
Yielding, if well played, finest music
To accompany the laughter of her eyes,
Spread our towels on the grass,
Gave our backs to the sun,
And lay for a long while without moving,
Like fillets under a broiler.
Then, as if dreaming, we rose from the grass
And eased our flesh into the river.

Oh! Cold! Oh là là! Cold!
The Dordogne gulped us,
Liquid wrapped us up;
We floated on the river's back,
Blue sky flowered in our eyes.

My sweet lady and I were together, though distinct;
Two, yet one.
We were like spirits, yet embodied.
We were perfectly out of our bodies
And perfectly in them.
The love permeating *being* enfolded us:
We were wholly given,
Wholly received;
Being beyond ourselves,
We were ourselves wholly.

I found myself a boy again in a wilderness river
Flanked by evergreen,
Embedded in silence.
In that primeval place,
In that other age,
I was young,
Forever young.
I floated in a blue vein of earth,

Life poured through me.

Here now a life later,
Floating in the Dordogne,
I am the same I,
Yet not the same.
It is like the layers of limestone in the cliff,
Bands laid down over eons,
Each in its place yet criss-crossed with others in a whole,
A work of time and seismic forces,
Like the life of any man or woman under the pressures
Of finitude and death,
The entail of foldings and tiltings and breakings,
The sediments of lime being what they were in the beginning,
Yet also altered,
Having been multiply reconfigured through the ages.

So in this time now,
At this stage of our course,
My beloved and I are floating in the Dordogne River,
Cradled by water.

Forget-me-nots are blooming in our eyes

And now we're on a dig in northern Galilee, Israel.
It is forty years ago, we're newly married,
We're at a site near the source of the Jordan River.
We're baking in the midday sun, turning into cakes.
Since dawn we've been digging for artifacts
From Rehoboam's breakaway kingdom:
I've been pounding rocks with a sledgehammer,
My beloved has been sifting dust.
At lunch-break we plunge into the Jordan River,
Near where it rises in the Anti-Lebanon Mountains.
The sky-blue water is crystal-pure, delicious.
We float in the headwaters ecstatically,
Sheltered by the motherly leaves of fig trees.

Someday we'll cross the Jordan one last time

In the Cirque de Montvalent in southern France,
Where the Dordogne River flows peacefully,
Summer swells,
The air is ripe with heat.
The cold water wrapping our bodies feels good.
Another band of life is claiming us,
The years are growing lean.
Above us now, as we float,
Stands the ancient cliff of limestone,

Pock-marked and furrowed,
Squinting at eternity.
No doubt it will stand till Christ returns and heals his world.
Then we shall plunge into the River of Life
That flows from the throne of God and of the Lamb.
My sweet lady and I,
Together with those who love God,
Will exult in the joy of our gracious Lord
And exalt His Name forever.

Suite III.4. The Campfire

Whispering in the great darkness beyond the campfire,
The needles of the black boughs sift the breath of night.
The marble moon floats in the firmament,
Its image gleams on the lake like a silver coin
Fallen through a hole in heaven's purse.
A fire blazes beneath a canvas tarp
Stretched wide between three trees.
Five men and a woman sit round the flames,
Inhaling on night's breath the smells of frying fish
And wood-smoke. In an iron pan on the logs,
Three trout caught that day sizzle and pop
In butter, their silver scales and rainbow bands
Browning slowly in the skillet. An owl hoots
In the dark woods, a loon calls on the lake;
Trees creak eerily, a branch rasps.
Wavelets at the water's edge lisp.

In all these sounds, what the six persons hear
Is silence. The soughing wind, the bird-calls,
The water softly lapping, these are the words

Of the wild earth, spoken out of utter stillness
To the listening ears of night.

The persons seated round the leaping flames
Are conscious of the silence underneath the sounds
Of night. They hear the Word underneath
The words spoken by the wild earth. Their ears
Are attuned to the presence of ineffable speech.
The breath whispering high up in the pine-tops
Kisses the stars that speckle heaven; it melts
The moon-coin on the lake, scattering silver; it stirs
The orange fire, makes shadows wobble on the tarp
And the rough-barked fir standing guard
On the six human beings eyeing the flames,
Of whom one, my father, tends the rainbow trout.
In the woods, creatures sleep or prowl: bear,
Deer, lynx, moose. The hooting owl
Watches on a branch; mice on the look-out
Twitch their noses; ants file up and down
The tree-trunks; bugs crawl among the roots.
Out on the lake the loon summons its mate.
A fish jumps. Splash. Silence. Night.

One

My father and stepmother, cousin John,
School-friend David, Al from England, and I,
Bonded as one in love,
Sit motionless around the leaping flames,
Beneath the taut tarp stretched between three trees.
Across the lake a round hill lifts its head
And casts its shadow on the water's face.
Clothed in fir, it contemplates the glow
On the other shore with wonder, as if the orange
Blaze in the middle of night were a sign
Of the fire at the heart of creation, the Life that makes
The moon roll round the sky, the owl hoot,
The moose crash in the underbrush, the loon
Call for its mate, the wavelets lick the shore.

The hill, considering these things, concludes
That it is so: the six silent figures
Seated round the burning logs, of whom one,
My father, is frying three fish for dinner,
Are indeed a sign of the Life at the heart of the world:
In the fullness of silence, Speech sounds;
In the fullness of night, Light flames.

To the stars, the moon, the enveloping forest,
To all the creatures in the wild earth,
The fir-clad hill, rising to the occasion,
Its shadow resting like a hand on the silver waters,
Declares an immemorial blessing:
"It is good, it is very good."

Suite III.5. The Stadium

We are here to love God,
All eighty thousand of us.
We are here to love God.
We're not here to tell the world we're important or unimportant,
We are here to love God.
He loved us first,
He is worthy of our love.
Beyond the cloud of unknowing,
Beyond the cloud of our ignorance,
He who is love, lives.
He is Lord!
How should we not declare our love to Him,
To Him who *is*,
The Spirit who is before all and made all?
He is the Breath who blows,
And lo—*Life!*

Tell me the ultimate Source
Of the eighty thousand people
Gathered here in this stadium
In the heart of the City of Man.

We come from everywhere on the planet,
East, West, South, North.
We come coloured black, white, brown,
But we make up one Body.
We belong to Him whom we love,
And to each other.
We thank God for bringing us to birth
After billions of years of travail.
We thank Him for the creatures we have charge of,
All creatures who run and swim and crawl and fly:
Pigs, eagles, dolphins, worms,
Bluebirds, tigers, whales, elephants,
Crows, guppies, camels,
Dogs, cats, horses;
And also for all mountains and lakes and oceans and rivers,
All plains and forests, trees and grasses,
All mushrooms, lichens, mosses,
All fruits, legumes, spices;
And for the sun and stars that cradle us,
The planets that accompany us in our annual course,
The moon that hallows night;
And for the flowers that paint the earth in summer
And the snow that whitens earth in winter.

We are here to praise God.
From where I am seated near the top of the stadium,
I see the tens of thousands of us lining the oval
Like successive strata in a canyon,
Down to the field and the bright stage at its centre,
Lit up now as evening falls
Like the pupil in the depths of an eye.
We are looking to God,
Our hearts long to behold him.

Way down on the stage there is activity.
A man comes forward to the microphone
And invites us to stand to thank God.
All eighty thousand of us rise.
"Father, thank you!" the man's voice rings out.
"Thank you, gracious God!"
Spontaneous applause goes up from the crowd:
"We thank you, Lord!" voices cry. "We praise you!"
Thousands of arms strain toward heaven.
"We praise you, we worship you!"

Now the instruments on the stage set to playing.
A medley swells in the twilight,
A cacophonic harmony,
Palpable, sweet, clamorous,
Like waves coming in off the sea
And breaking disparately over reefs.

Again I see activity on the stage.
The man at the microphone raises his arm
And points into the night.
A hush falls suddenly over the stadium,
As when a cloudburst ceases all at once
And pelting rain abruptly stops.
"Behold the Lamb!" cries the man,
Pointing into the night.
"Behold the Lamb who stands beside the throne of God!"

As if from an infinite distance,
The sweetest singing ever heard
Falls upon our ears. The sound is like silk
And is textured like water
Dropping from a great height into a pool.
Surely our ecstatic singing
Is an echo of this heavenly choir!

And lo! We descry a figure clothed in white,
Blazing like a star in the firmament,
A Lamb standing as though it had been slain.

"Behold the Lamb of God, who takes away the sins of the world!"

A prayer pierces the dark from one corner of the stadium.
"Father, show your mercy! Forgive us our sins!"
And from another:
"Yes, Lord: forgive us as we forgive those who hate us!"
Now with power God's Spirit comes in like a tide.
Supplications ripple through the stadium
Like gusts of wind through a wheatfield.
Joyful singing starts up again,
Bursts of light flaring in the night like fireworks.
For minutes it goes on;
God fills us with his Breath;
He makes our hearts His dwelling place.

At last there is silence again,
Broken only by receding sounds
Of honking cars and sirens in the City of Man.
A deep peace falls upon the multitude.

The man on the stage comes forward
And speaks into the microphone softly:
"We are not worthy, Lord,
But you love us.
Eternal Son of the Father,
You became one of us,
You revealed to us the Father.
You came to bring us home to Him,
You are the Door to His great House,
Through you we are His sons and daughters.
You made us for yourself,
You loved us unto death.
You redeemed us,
We are yours forever.
Lord, receive our love in return.
In you is all our hope."
He pauses.
Then he speaks again, strongly:
"Glory be to the Lamb!
Glory be to the Lamb who was slain and is alive!"
He raises high his arms to the Lamb,
All of us raise high our arms to the Lamb.
Together eighty thousand voices roar:
"Glory to the Lamb who was slain and is alive!"

Made in the USA
Middletown, DE
23 December 2017